Gunther

James Kaine

HORROR HOUSE PUBLISHING

ISBN: 979-8-9867312-6-1 (eBook), 979-8-9867312-8-5 (Paperback), 979-8-9867312-9-2 (Hardcover)

Cover design by: Damonza.com

A QUICK NOTE

Hello and thank you for picking up this copy of *Gunther!*

Before you dive in, I wanted to let you know – in case you didn't already – that this book is a prequel to my novel, *My Pet Werewolf.* While the events of this story take place prior to the start of the novel, there are some minor spoilers, particularly in the epilogue. My recommendation is to start with *MPW*, but you can easily enjoy *Gunther* on its own, so feel free to jump right in, I just know some readers like to go in completely blind to a story's twists and turns.

If you would rather read *My Pet Werewolf* first, you can get a copy wherever books are sold!

But, however you choose to read, I hope you enjoy!

-James

CHAPTER 1

On the night Dr. David Bixby's life changed forever, he was working the night shift in the emergency room at St. Theresa's Medical Center in Jacksonville, Florida.

At thirty-two years old, David was in his prime. Standing six-foot, one inch tall, he was in excellent shape, the result of a steady workout regimen. It wasn't always easy keeping up with it, especially when he found himself stuck on double shifts in the ER, but it was precisely those physical demands that spurred him to maintain his fitness level. He stuck to a healthy diet comprising lean proteins, ample servings of green vegetables, and limited processed carbohydrates even though he absolutely loved processed carbohydrates. After all who wouldn't opt for a donut over a salad? He kept his alcohol intake low to avoid dulling effects on his body or mind, but damn if he didn't need a Scotch after some of the tougher nights in the emergency room.

He also took great care to keep up his appearance. His hair was always neatly styled and, not being a fan of facial hair, he shaved every single day to keep his face smooth and clean while he was interacting with patients or colleagues.

David's attention to detail in his appearance was not an aberration. He took great care in everything he did, a necessity since he often found himself with people's lives in his hands, sometimes literally. Anything less than full attention could be the difference between life and death. It was an obligation David took on with the utmost seriousness, even when he wasn't on call.

On one occasion five years ago, David was attending the Easter Vigil service at his local parish. He was twenty-six years old and fresh out of medical school and had just started his residency. He was with his parents and girlfriend observing Mass when he heard a heavy thud behind him. Without a second's hesitation, he ran back and sifted through a growing crowd of onlookers to find an elderly woman had collapsed into the pew. As the priest dutifully continued the liturgy, trying to distract the congregation from the spectacle, David furiously worked on the woman, performing CPR until the ambulance arrived.

Unfortunately, the woman, an eighty-three-year-old widow who had been attending the Mass with her daughter, passed away en route to the hospital. It devastated David to learn the news. Even though there was nothing he could have done, his inability to save her still bothered him. That was the man Dr. David Bixby was. He lived to serve his community.

Of course, there were those who thought him too good to be true. Tall, smart, handsome and with such a strong sense of civic duty? There had to be something wrong with him, right? Nobody's perfect, and David certainly had his fair share of flaws, but he was a good, caring man and well-liked by all who know him.

The night the stranger was rolled into the ER was in late June. It had been strikingly humid in Jacksonville that week, coming off a series of early summer thunderstorms. For most of the day, it had been sunny, but the clouds came rolling in just after 5 p.m. and the skies darkened under their cover.

Now, it was almost 10:30. David, having worked his third night shift in a row due to an unfortunate bout of stomach flu that had rendered Dr. Jenkins incapacitated for the better part of a week, was trying to blink away his tiredness. While he typically avoided coffee once the afternoon rolled around, tonight he carried a steaming Styrofoam cup of java. He took it black tonight. Despite his desire to maintain his health, he loved his coffee with cream and sugar. But, seeing as all they had in the break room was that weird powder creamer, he opted to forego the pleasure for the caffeinating effect.

He had just finished up attending to a young man who had broken his wrist attempting an ill-advised stunt on his skateboard. X-rays showed a relatively clean break, so he called for a cast to be put on and informed the boy and his mother that they'd be released shortly after.

David thanked God that it had turned out to be a slow evening. The past few nights, he'd felt like every time he finished seeing one patient, two more rolled in. He'd dealt with heart attacks, unexplained abdominal pains, the aforementioned broken bones, and one poor soul who had been struck by a car in a hit-and-run.

They say variety is the spice of life, but Dr. Bixby had had more than his fill over the past seventy-two hours.

David walked behind the long circular desk that took up the center of the emergency room. He found a chair and sat down, melting back into it as he took a tentative sip of the scalding liquid. Sure, coffee was meant to be hot, but was it really supposed to be *this* hot?

"Stealing my chair, I see?" a woman's voice said from behind him.

He spun in the chair and saw Jenna Fleming standing in front of him, wearing a wry smile.

Jenna was a registered nurse who had started at St. Theresa's six months ago. She was twenty-six years old and had recently moved to Jacksonville with her boyfriend from North Carolina after he had finished his military service.

David would be lying if he tried to say she wasn't an extremely attractive woman. Standing about five foot four and in great shape, toned but still maintaining a healthy amount of curve, her scrubs unable to do much to hide the shapely figure underneath. She typically kept her long, strawberry blonde hair out of the way in a tight ponytail. She always wore some makeup, but not much, her natural features not requiring enhancement.

Jenna probably caught the eye of most she came across. It didn't help that she was also a huge flirt, especially, it seemed, with David. If he were single, he may have played along. He broke more than a few hearts throughout college and med school, but he had long since settled down, having been happily married, to Amy Davenport, the aforementioned girlfriend from the evening at church, for the past two and a half years. Even if he had never been a model boyfriend in past relationships, that all changed when he met Amy during his last year at Johns Hopkins. He had been a one-woman man since then, despite the occasional effort of the Jennas of the world to get him to stray.

He offered Jenna an apologetic smile and stood. "All yours."

"You talking about the chair?" she said with a wink.

"I am," he said, offering as polite an eye roll as possible, acknowledging the flirting without engaging.

"Oh," Jenna said in mock disappointment as she slinked into the now-vacant chair. Well, half of it was mock. She had tried flirting with the handsome doctor on multiple occasions since she started. David knew she had a serious boyfriend and had to believe that she was just trying to get a rise out of him rather than seriously suggesting mutual infidelity. Still, he wondered how she would behave if he reciprocated, even though he had no intention of doing so. He suspected her relationship wasn't on the most solid of footing, having seen her come in on more than one occasion looking like she'd been crying. Co-workers had also observed her engaged in what appeared to be some pretty intense conversations while on her phone outside the building.

He felt for her, but it didn't matter if she was serious or not. Even if Jenna's flirting was more than just playful, he couldn't imagine being unfaithful to his wife.

As if on cue, Jenna asked him, "How's your wife doing?"

David smiled, never wanting to pass up a chance to talk her up. "Amazing!" he beamed. "She just finished up the school year, so now we can focus on the last few things we need to do to get the house ready before the baby arrives in September."

His smile widened as he remembered the past weekend when he and Amy had finished painting the nursery. She had playfully dabbed the blue paint on the tip of his nose before planting a kiss on his lips, the paint smudging her own as she did. This week he had planned out a whole day where he was going to take her for a massage in the morning, followed by lunch and a trip to the outlets to get the last few things they needed to complete the baby's room. All Amy knew was that they were going shopping. She didn't know he planned to pamper her along the way. He couldn't wait to see her face light up when they got to the spa.

Jenna stuck out her lower lip and nodded in what appeared to be legitimate admiration. "She made it all the way through the school year with a bunch of rabid kindergarteners while pregnant? I'm impressed."

"She's an impressive woman."

"Well," she said, giving him a look over. "I suppose she'd have to be."

"Thank you for asking," David said, feeling a little awkward about the entire exchange. Time to shift back to business. "I think everyone is pretty well settled at this point. Let's just hope there're no more surprises in store for us tonight."

David regretted the utterance almost immediately because no sooner did it escape his lips than the bay doors flew open and a pair of EMTs—Jack, a husky ex-football player from Florida State whose NFL dreams were dashed by ACL tears in two consecutive seasons, and Ziggy, a Nashville-imported metalhead with tattoos covering most visible parts of her body—wheeled in a stretcher.

The stretcher's occupant was a tall, gangly man who was thrashing violently as the techs tried their damnedest to keep him on the stretcher. He had long stringy hair that would probably hang down to his shoulders. It was greasy and matted with God knows what smeared in places. Long strands clung to the man's sweaty, stubble-covered face.

He was barefoot and the bottoms of his feet were filthy and covered in screaming red blisters. His jeans were tattered and ragged, hanging loose off of his thin frame. He wore a formerly white button-down shirt that had yellowed over time and was now torn open. Jack was holding pressure with a gloved hand on a stack of gauze over the man's exposed chest, the white material soaked through with blood.

"Put him in six," David said, pointing to the empty bay as he rushed around the desk to meet the EMTs while slipping on his gloves. "What do we have here?"

"Gunshot wound," Ziggy said. "Found him behind Josie's when someone heard shots and called it in."

The man let out a guttural scream, wet and choked as blood filled his throat. He thrust his upper torso up off the gurney in an attempt to escape, but the doctor and the EMTs held him down with some effort. David was shocked at how strong the man was, especially in his condition.

They rolled him toward the bed. Ziggy got on one side of the stretcher while Jack remained on the other. Each pulled their section of the blanket taut and lifted the man, with great effort, onto the bed.

Jack pushed the stretcher out of the way as David made his way around to the other side of the bed and pulled out the small light in his pocket. He flicked it on and shone one in each of the injured man's eyes.

"Pupils are dilated. Did he take something?"

"No clue," Ziggy said.

The man kept thrashing about, making it difficult for David to assess his condition.

"Hold him down!" He instructed Jack and Ziggy. "Jenna! I need a sedative! Get me two milligrams of propofol now!"

The EMTs did as instructed and Jenna entered the room within seconds with a syringe ready to go. David took it and injected the man in one of the bulging veins in his neck. The medication worked fast and the man slumped back on the bed, although he continued to moan, his head lolling back and forth on the bed.

David moved the gauze and immediately blood poured out of the small, circular hole in his chest. But the main thing that hit David at that moment was the smell. The wound emitted an odor akin to rotten eggs. It was putrid and nearly made the doctor gag. He'd seen and smelled some truly awful things during his time in the ER, but he couldn't recall ever smelling anything worse than the stench emanating from the hole in this man's chest.

As David looked the victim over, he found more anomalies. The edges of the wound appeared to be burned, as if someone had tried to cauterize it. There were also red blotches spreading outward from the cavity. He'd seen a few shootings during his tenure, but he'd never seen a bullet do anything like this. Had it been coated in something? Like when some native tribes would cover their arrowheads in feces so that infection would kill their adversaries, even if the projectile itself didn't?

He pushed the gauze back over the wound and called for the nurses to prep the operating room. He knew he needed to get the bullet out if he was to have any chance of saving this man.

"The moon... the moon..." the man said weakly.

"Sir," David said, disregarding the rambling. "You've been shot, but we're going to take care of you. Do you understand me?"

"Not time... the moon is... not time..."

He was incoherent. David saw that his eyes had rolled back in his head, just the bloodshot pupils visible from his vantage point. The man was feverish and soaked in sweat. David could feel the heat radiating from his body.

"We need to move him. Now!" He said as the man continued to rant.

"When the moon is full... I'll be back. When the moon is full."

"What the hell is he saying?" Jack asked.

"It doesn't matter, we need to—"

David didn't get to finish the sentence as the man bolted up on the bed, causing David to slip away and release his pressure on the wound. Blood spurted out and splattered on Ziggy's shirt. She was clearly repulsed but, to her credit, she followed her training and kept her focus.

"Help me hold him!" David cried, trying to push the man back down.

He only got him about a third of the way back to the bed when the man pushed him back and clamped his teeth down hard on David's hand. David shouted in pain as the man bit harder, his rotten yellowed teeth pushing through the latex material of the doctor's glove and sinking into the flesh below.

"Shit!" David yelled as Jack and Ziggy grabbed the man and shoved him back down onto the bed. He pushed his way up one last time and unleashed a stream of vomit tinged heavily with blood. He soaked the bottom of the bed and the floor below. The volume of puke was staggering, unlike anything these medical professionals had seen in their lives. When he finally stopped spewing, he collapsed back onto the mattress, his arms falling over the sides and his feet dangling over the edge of the bed that was too small to completely accommodate his lanky frame. He violently convulsed one last time, then fell still with one last oddity coming to the staff's attention when a plume of smoke rose from the wound.

David retrieved a towel from the cabinet in the corner of the room and pressed it against his hand, which was bleeding pretty significantly. He wiped away the plasma and observed the wound, seeing the imprints of the man's teeth in the flesh. The skin was jagged and torn. He was going to need stitches.

He covered the injury back up and looked at Jenna, who was standing back in shock at what they'd all just witnessed.

"Jenna," he said calmly. She didn't answer. "Jenna!"

The dumbfounded nurse snapped out of her trance and focused her attention on David.

"Check his vitals."

She popped her stethoscope in her ears and hesitantly approached the motionless figure. David couldn't blame her. After what happened to him, she must be terrified that he would pop up again. But she fought through any trepidation she may have felt and placed the chestpiece above the man's heart. She moved it around, searching for cardiac activity. She looked at David and shook her head, silently confirming that there was none.

David moved over to the other side of the bed; his injured hand wrapped in the towel. He held it against his blood-stained coat and used his other to grip the man around his wrist and raise it up. It took a little effort, but he got his fingers on the proper spot to check for a pulse. Again, there was none. He gently lowered the man's hand to the bed and placed it at his side respectfully rather than just letting it drop to the floor.

He looked at his watch.

"Time of death—10:38 p.m."

CHAPTER 2

David found himself in the atypical position of being a patient in the hospital where he worked. He guessed it wasn't that unusual. Doctors got sick too. But this was the first time he'd been injured while on the job in the ER.

The first order of business, once the scene had calmed down, was to get a post-exposure prophylaxis shot as a precaution against rabies. David couldn't help but be irritated knowing that he would need to get three more PEP injections at three, seven and fourteen days from now, but it was better than the alternative of, you know, getting rabies. From the state of the man who bit him, that may be an actual possibility. Fortunately, any side effects from the shots were typically mild, especially in someone as healthy as he was.

He sat on the bed in bay number two, across from what was now a crime scene in bay number six. Jenna sat on a stool in front of him, threading a needle through his numbed hand as she stitched the wound closed.

"You're not even flinching," she remarked.

It hadn't really occurred to him. It was a little

14

uncomfortable, but the lidocaine was doing its job. He shrugged as Jenna smiled at him.

"You're very brave," she said.

David returned the smile but dialed it back. "I wouldn't be much of a doctor if I got squeamish over stitches."

She laughed. "That's not what I mean. The way you rushed over to help that man. Even as out of control as he was. Even after he fucking bit you..."

David gave her a look. She rolled her eyes and continued.

"You just had a patient try to eat you before vomiting blood all over the room. I'd think a f-bomb or two would be understandable, wouldn't you agree?"

He couldn't help but laugh. Yes, decorum wasn't really a top concern at this point. "I guess so," he agreed.

She finished the task and cut the thread with a small pair of scissors before wrapping his hand. When she was done, she held his hand in hers. She made like she was trying to examine it, but held it a little too long for David's comfort. When she rubbed her thumb over the back of his hand, he withdrew it as if the gesture hurt. An awkward silence hung over them for a second before David broke it.

"Thank you."

"You're welcome," she said, holding eye contact, again just long enough to make David uneasy. The silence hung for a few moments before David changed the subject.

"Excuse me, Dr. Bixby?" a man's voice came from behind Jenna.

David looked over her shoulder to see two uniformed police officers standing in the entry to the bay. One was short and stout, looking to be in his forties, his uniform shirt stretched out by a moderate beer belly. His name tag read *Sgt. Taft*. The other was young and lean. Not too tall, but taller than his partner. His clean-shaven face made him look like a teenager, but David guessed his actual age was probably mid-twenties. His name plate read *P.O. Vance*.

"Yes, sir," David said to Taft, who was the one he assumed had addressed him.

Taft looked at the fresh bandage on the David's hand.

"We're just taking statements as to what happened here," Taft informed him. "Are you okay with talking now? You can always come by the station tomorrow if you prefer."

He did not. Tomorrow he was going to catch up on sleep and be lazy for once.

"No, sir," David said. "I'm fine talking with you gentlemen now." He nodded toward Jenna. "Jenna, can you excuse us?"

She actually looked hurt as she finished wrapping his hand, but got up and left without protest. Maybe he was just tired and loopy from blood loss, but he made a mental note to dial back his already measured interactions with the young nurse. For whatever reason, she didn't seem to get the hint that he wasn't interested.

"Dr. Bixby," Sergeant Taft said, eyeing the freshly bandaged wound, "Is it correct that the man with the gunshot wound inflicted that injury on you?"

"Yes," David answered. "He was violent and difficult to restrain. He jumped up and bit me before succumbing to his wounds."

"Did you observe any injuries other than the gunshot wound?"

David thought about it for a second. "There was some unusual blistering that I'm not too sure about. In fact, the gunshot wound itself was... odd."

"Odd how?" Officer Vance asked.

"The skin around the bullet was burned. It was almost as if he'd been stabbed with a burning poker or a similar object. I've seen gunshot wounds before, but nothing like this. It even continued to smoke after the patient had expired."

The cops exchanged a glance, looking just as confused by the situation as David was.

"Was there any evidence of tampering with the bullet or the area of impact?" Taft asked.

David shook his head. "Not that I could see. He died before we could extract the bullet. If there was anything else, I'm guessing the medical examiner will find it."

"Anything else you can recall?" Taft continued. "Have

you ever seen that man before?"

"No. Never. Who was he?"

Vance chimed in. "No identification. Could be a drifter."

"He was shot near Josie's Bar? On Whittaker?" David asked.

Taft answered. "They found him in the alley. Patrons heard loud bangs that some described as gunshots. One of the kitchen staff investigated and found this man in the alley and called 911. EMTs got there quickly and transported him here. We were a few minutes behind. By the time we got here, everything was over."

"And you have no idea who did this to him?" David asked.

"We don't have any suspects yet. The worker told us he had just found the man. No one else was in the vicinity."

David didn't know what to make of all of this. The victim's attack on him wasn't any more than a violent outburst of a dying man. He had nothing to do with why this apparent vagrant was shot. David had simply been in the wrong place at the wrong time.

Still, the circumstances were strange. The man had a manic strength about him, one that David had seen in patients before, but never quite to this level. Plus, the weird burn marks, the sulfuric odor, the copious amount of bloody vomit. All of it was very unusual for a gunshot wound to the chest. This was one patient who was going to stay burned in his memory for quite some time.

"Dr. Bixby?" Sergeant Taft's voice broke him out of his thoughts.

"Yes, Sergeant?"

"Anything else you can think of?"

"No."

CHAPTER 3

David felt something pulse under the palm of his hand, not thinking too much of it at first, still caught between the sleeping and waking worlds.

He would have typically finished the night shift at 6 a.m., but because of his injuries, the hospital called in Dr. Halloran who, although she was none too pleased with having to come in during her vacation, was sympathetic and understanding once she was apprised of the situation. She got to the hospital and was ready to go just before midnight, at which point David could head home.

Amy was almost certainly asleep, so David didn't want to call her and interrupt her rest, opting for a simple text message so as not to alarm her if he walked in unannounced in the middle of the night. She didn't respond, so David assumed she had turned in for the night.

When he got home, he took care to lock his car manually rather than risking the beep of the remote, a courtesy to his wife and his neighbors. He carefully made his way in, trying to minimize the creaking of the door and clicking of the locks. The house was dark, save for the oven light that Amy always left on when David was working nights, providing him with some illumination in case he got home before the sun came up. He slipped his shoes off by the door and shuffled into the kitchen to turn it off.

He made it upstairs and into their bedroom without rousing his sleeping spouse. It comforted him to hear her light snoring, a recent development as she moved into her third trimester. Once in the comfort of his bedroom, David stripped down and placed his clothes in the hamper specially designated for Dr. Bixby's work clothes. At that point, he sneaked into the shower and thoroughly washed himself to remove the stains of the night's events.

Once he finished showering, David changed his bandage, not taking too long to examine the wound itself, a task better served for the morning, before tiptoeing to bed and gingerly crawling in, successful in his attempt to keep Amy asleep. He was out almost immediately after hitting the pillow.

A while later, he wasn't exactly sure how long, he felt another pulse as he realized his uninjured palm was resting on a smooth surface. Skin. He felt a slight weight on the back of his hand. Another hand.

He opened his eyes and saw Amy looking at him, a

twinkle in her hazel eyes. Her dirty blonde hair was messy with bed head and splayed across the fabric of the headboard as she sat upright. She wore a pink shirt with the cheeky inscription *Future MILF*. Her sister had gotten it for her as a joke. She had no intention of wearing it outside of the house, but it was certainly amusing enough to use as a sleep shirt. The fabric was bunched up over her ample belly. She smiled and squeezed David's hand that she had placed on her exposed tummy.

"Someone wanted to say good morning," she whispered. "He's been very active since I woke up."

David felt another pulse and smiled back at his wife; at this moment, last night's events were a distant memory. Even with all his medical training and experience, he still marveled when he felt his son gently kick from his mother's womb.

He sat up and smiled at her.

"Good morning, baby."

"Good morning," Amy replied.

"What time is it?"

"Seven-thirty. What time did you get in?"

"A little before one," David said, bringing his other hand back, running it through his hair.

Amy nodded to the bandage. "Can I assume your early exit and bandaged hand are related?"

"They are," David replied. "There was an incident."

Amy's smile fully dropped and she looked concerned.

"What kind of incident?"

He recounted the entire story to her. The gunshot victim, the bite, the cops. He didn't go into gory detail, but he always wanted to be honest with his wife.

"Oh, my God," she said. "Does it hurt?"

As he smiled to reassure her, his pain receptors ironically took the cue and fired throughout the wound. He did his best not to wince.

"It does, but I'm okay. They gave me a shot as a precaution. I'm going to stop back in this afternoon to get a full blood panel worked up, just to make sure."

"Babe..."

"It's all good," David reassured her. "Just a hazard of the occupation. I'll only be an hour or two."

He got up out of bed and went into the bathroom, taking a moment to look at himself in the mirror. His color was off and bags sat under his bloodshot eyes. Neither of these was a surprise as he'd been pushing himself pretty hard this past week, but he made a mental note to dial it back, especially with the baby only a few months away.

David carefully unwrapped his hand and looked over the injury. To his surprise, it didn't look too bad at all. Jenna had done a good job stitching him up, and while there was bruising, it was pretty minimal. The bite had been decently deep, so he expected more trauma based on the state of the man, but he guessed he shouldn't be upset that it wasn't as bad as it could have been.

Wrapping it back up, David used his other hand to splash some water on his face, gently patting it dry with a towel before exiting the bathroom with a smile.

"How about breakfast?" he asked Amy.

CHAPTER 4

After breakfast, David and Amy took a walk around the block. The couple enjoyed regular strolls together, especially as Amy's pregnancy progressed, taking the opportunity to get regular exercise. They had bought their house in the idyllic suburban neighborhood eighteen months before, fully intending to fill the three additional bedrooms with children in the coming years.

They kept the conversation light, neither of them wanting to mention David's injury. And why would they? As far as they were concerned, it was an isolated incident. A scary one, sure, but also an occupational hazard. David would get his blood and saliva tested and finish the course of vaccine treatment and it would soon be little more than a crazy workplace story to share at dinner parties. Well, maybe *after* dinner.

When they rounded the corner and reached their front porch, David blew Amy a kiss, not wanting to risk anything physical until he knew he was in the clear of any type of communicable infection. He bade her goodbye and drove to St. Theresa's.

When he arrived, he headed straight to the lab. Andre was on duty. A lanky black kid, he was working as a lab tech while putting himself through college with an eye on med school. David liked Andre and was always willing to give him advice or guidance when needed. He was also a huge pro wrestling fan; a form of entertainment Dr. Bixby hadn't had interest in since he was a teenager. The tech was watching the latest episode of *AEW Dynamite* on his phone when David entered the room.

"Is Bret Hart still the champ?" David asked playfully, knowing all too well that Bret had retired in the early 2000s, right around the time he lost interest in the product.

Andre gave him the stink eye and a sarcastic response: "Yeah. He's defending against Koko B. Ware next weekend."

"Oh, yeah," David played along. "He the one with the snake?"

"Man, stop playing with me. You know that's Jake *the Snake* Roberts. Koko had the parrot."

David laughed. "Yeah, yeah."

"What can I do for you, Doc?" Andre asked. "Heard about that business in the ER last night. You good?"

"Yeah, I'm good," David said with a nod. "Or, at least, I hope I am." He held up his bandaged hand. "I need a full blood panel and a saliva test."

***

Fifteen minutes later, Andre had the samples and was getting them analyzed. With some time to kill, David took the elevator to the basement. Conveniently, the hospital had a satellite office for the County Medical Examiner and the receptionist had informed him that the ME was, in fact, on site at the moment, saving David a trip to the main office across town.

As he entered the sterile examination room, he saw Gary Steinmann, the chief medical examiner, standing over a body covered in a sheet. It was too small to cover the body completely and the legs were sticking out further than usual.

Gary was short, only about five foot eight, but he was in excellent shape for a guy in his mid-fifties. David guessed that when you saw that many dead bodies in the course of your job, it was an excellent motivator to keep yourself healthy.

Next to the ME stood another man. He was taller than Gary, but shorter than David. He was wearing a wrinkled black-and-white pin-striped suit and a fedora that, while not quite matching, was still complimentary. The man held a heavy-looking peacoat over his folded elbow, a garment that was very odd considering the stifling Florida heat.

The man was the first to notice David. Gary followed

a second later.

"Ah!" Gary said. "Dr. Bixby."

The man eyed David up and down. His eyes were narrow and severe, visible even through the tinted spectacles he wore. He reminded the doc of Judge Doom from *Who Framed Roger Rabbit?*, one of his favorite movies from childhood, even though it came out a few years before he was even born. David approached cautiously.

"This is Detective..."

"Chaney," the man replied, not giving Gary a chance to complete the introduction.

David saw Gary frown as he extended his hand to greet Detective Chaney. The man had an accent that he couldn't quite place. Definitely American, but not from the South.

The man didn't accept, instead nodding toward David's bandaged hand.

"Is that the bite inflicted by the deceased?"

David dropped his hand, giving up on the greeting.

"Yes, sir," he replied.

"How is it?"

How are YOU would be more polite, David thought.

"It's actually okay. Looked worse last night."

Something about that didn't seem to sit right with Chaney.

"So, it's healing quickly, would you say?"

David looked to Gary, who only offered a subtle shrug.

"Don't know about that. It just looked worse before I got patched up. Not too uncommon with these types of injuries."

"And how would you say you're feeling overall?"

I guess you do have some manners.

"Not bad, considering. I'm getting labs done to make sure he didn't give me anything, but overall, I feel okay."

Chaney said nothing further, but held his gaze too long to be comfortable. What was he getting at?

"I guess you came down here for the rundown on this guy?" Gary asked, breaking the tension. David looked over Chaney's shoulder.

"That's right," he acknowledged. "You find anything?"

Chaney finally broke the stare and turned his attention to the ME.

"Okay, so we still don't have an ID, but he was the victim of a single gunshot wound," Gary explained. "But I can't say for sure that's what killed him."

David didn't seem surprised. "Blood poisoning?" he asked.

Gary nodded and pulled the sheet back over the man's head, resting it just below his shoulder blades. He looked like he'd been dead a lot longer than the approximately eighteen hours David knew had passed since he'd expired.

The skin was a pale, milky white. There were red

blotches spread across what David could see, but he imagined the rest of the body would look the same. The man's lips were blue and curled outward, exposing rotted, yellow teeth. It was a gnarly sight, but David had seen sepsis before. While this was certainly an extreme case, it wasn't unheard of.

The young doctor tensed up. If this man had something in his blood, that upped the chances that he'd passed something along through the bite. David shook the thought away. His bloodwork was being processed. He'd know soon.

"So, what about the wound? It looked... scorched."

Gary responded by lowering the sheet further, placing it under the corpse's sternum this time, exposing the bullet hole. It wasn't a large hole and had the requisite bruising around the radius, but there was definitely something weird. The skin around the crater was blackened, as if burned by something very hot. He even got a whiff of smoke coming off of the cavity. Any gunshot he had seen previously wasn't like this.

"Any idea what kind of gun would do something like that?" Chaney asked.

"You tell me, Detective," Gary responded. "I'm not a munitions expert."

Chaney cleared his throat but didn't answer. There was definitely something off about him.

"Do you have any idea who he is or who did this to

him?" David chimed in.

"No," the detective answered curtly.

The three stood in an awkward silence for several moments until Gary offered, "Is there anything else we can do for you, Detective?"

"No."

***

David talked to Gary for a few more minutes, but there was nothing else to learn from the corpse right now. The investigators would perform toxicology tests, but they would take a week or two to get the results. They both noted the oddness of Detective Chaney but wrote it off as little more than a quirky personality.

After leaving the exam room, David returned to the lab where Andre was waiting with his results.

"All clear, Doc," he confirmed. "But I'm sure you know it can take a few days for certain things to show up, so get tested again in about a week."

David nodded, knowing from the start that was what he would have to do. "Thanks, Andre."

As David made his way through the halls and to the exit, he saw a tall, slender brunette woman in a navy-blue pantsuit with a white button-down top approaching him. A golden badge was affixed to her belt, and he saw the holstered handgun on her hip as the jacket swayed with her gait.

"Dr. Bixby?" she asked, handing him a card that read *Detective Allison Burkhardt, Jacksonville P.D.*

"Yes, ma'am?" David acknowledged. "How can I help you?"

"I'm investigating the shooting last night. I understand you were the doctor on call and that you had an interaction with the man?" she said, nodding toward his bandaged wrist.

David was confused. "Are you working with Detective Chaney on the case?"

"I'm sorry, who?"

CHAPTER 5

A week had passed since David's bite. He went to the hospital that morning to get his third PEP shot with just one more needed to complete the course. Unexpectedly, he also got his stitches out that morning too. Typically, they would stay in for two weeks, but David had noticed the skin growing in over them, a surefire sign that they had been in place too long.

Dr. Halloran marveled at just how quickly the wound was healing. "You may very well be the healthiest person on Earth!" she joked. David laughed along, but he understood how the healing process worked, and the quickness with which the injury was disappearing was definitely weird.

After that, he went up to the lab to see Andre. The tech was deep in one of his textbooks when David walked in. A quick blood draw, followed by a brief wait, showed no sign of rabies or any other concerns. Despite his relative confidence that he was in the clear, he was still relieved to hear the news.

That made him excited for the next shot even more.

As a precaution, he had avoided all intimacy with Amy since the incident. They had always been an affectionate couple, so not even being able to kiss her was borderline maddening. Beyond that, he also found himself extremely aroused much of the time. More so than usual, even with a healthy sex drive. It took everything he had some nights not to throw caution out the window and just fuck his wife. Maybe it was simply the fact that he knew he couldn't that was stoking his desire, but never in his life could he remember being so horny.

One more week, he told himself. He knew Amy was feeling it too. Maybe not necessarily the sex, but definitely the closeness. Until then, he would just have to take matters into his own hands in the shower, as had become a daily routine for him.

As he left the hospital, he called Amy. Before he left, he promised to pick up Chinese food on the way home, so now he just needed to take her order. She requested house lo mein, crab Rangoon and wonton soup. David knew it frustrated her not to add sushi, but that was a pregnancy no-no. He promised he'd take her out for it the first chance they had once the baby was born.

Their favorite spot for this type of cuisine was Mr. China, a small, cozy joint in the same shopping center where they picked up their weekly groceries. They were quick and efficient. David always marveled at how Helen, the woman who took the orders and dealt with the customers, never asked for a name or gave him a number, yet somehow always knew which order was whose.

When David pulled up to the restaurant, he saw inside that there were two people waiting, one at the counter and one a respectable distance behind. The person at the counter was a wispy, middle-aged woman whose bob was badly in need of a new dye job. The other patron was a tired-looking man about David's age, wearing a wrinkled suit with his tie loosened and top shirt button undone. He looked like he wanted nothing more than to grab his food and get the hell out of there.

As he walked up to take his spot in line, David noticed that the woman's raised voice and animated gestures. She was really laying into Helen. Helen wasn't actually her name, but, like many immigrants, she'd opted for an Americanized version for her customers. To her credit, she was listening and nodding, trying to address the customer's concerns, but to no avail.

"Is your job really this hard?" the woman asked. "How difficult is it to get an order right?"

"Ma'am, you order pint, not quart," Helen responded evenly. "But it okay, we fix for you."

"I ordered the *bigger* one," the woman retorted.

"You order pint," the server said, again not getting flustered. "Quart is bigger."

In all the years David had patronized this

establishment, they had never once made a mistake with his order, no matter how complex. Plus, the fact that the woman said she ordered the *bigger* one and not a *quart* was convincing evidence that she was the one who had made the error, not Helen.

"You can't even speak proper English and you're telling me I'm the one that's wrong?" the woman spat out with venom. "What can I do to get through to you people?"

That sent a bolt of rage through David's body. Before he could register what he was doing, the words escaped his mouth. "You can try not being a total fucking bitch."

The woman spun around and looked at David, eyes bulging. He could actually see a vein popping out of her forehead. Suit Guy in front of him turned as well, his look one of *I can't believe you just said that*.

"And just who the hell do you think you are?" the woman asked.

"I'm a hungry customer waiting to pick up his order but is being held up by a Karen who can't take responsibility for fucking up her own order."

David cringed internally. He never used this much profanity. Besides that, he never used *Karen* as a pejorative. He actually had a cousin named Karen, so he didn't see the name as a negative. But he just couldn't control himself. It was like some deep anger prompted him to confront this woman.

"Fuck you," the lady said.

David saw red and took a step forward, almost colliding with Suit Guy. "No, fuck you, you entitled cunt."

What the hell was that? Cunt? David didn't think he'd ever said that word aloud in his life.

"How dare you?" she said, taking a step back and bumping the counter.

"It okay," Helen said, trying to defuse the situation.

"No," David replied. "It's not okay."

He stepped around Suit Guy and approached the woman.

"If you touch me, I'll sue," she said, her voice cracking.

"Don't flatter yourself. You have two options. Either apologize to this nice lady behind the counter, get your food and get out. Or you can just get the fuck out now."

The woman turned to Helen, who said nothing but confirmed with her eyes that those were her only two options. She turned back to David and he saw the fight draining out of her. She clutched her purse and stormed out of the restaurant, giving David a wide berth as she did. He watched as she pushed the door open, the small bell at the top clanging with the motion. She turned back and shouted.

"The food here sucks anyway! I'm leaving a one star review on Yelp!"

David glared at her and she gulped before hurrying away, the door shutting behind her. He was pretty sure she would never actually write that review.

He looked at Helen apologetically. Not just because of the harassment she had experienced, but also out of remorse for his own behavior, which was more likely the reason she looked rattled right now. She had surely dealt with more than her fair share of customers who were rude, racist, or both. However, to see a regular behaving so out of character was likely a little jarring.

"Sorry, Helen," he said. "Let me pay for the food she left."

"Unnecessary."

"I insist. Ring it up with mine after you help this gentleman here." He turned to Suit Guy and saw the uncomfortable look on his face. That raised that anger again. "You got a problem now?"

Suit Guy put up his hands in a non-threatening gesture. "Nope. All good, man."

He cautiously stepped around David and paid for his order, getting out of there as quick as he could. Once he was gone, David walked up to the counter, paid for both his food and the woman's, leaving a sizable tip on top of everything. He was calmer now and felt bad about how he had reacted. Sure, the woman was an asshole, but David typically reacted to contentious situations with more grace than he had tonight.

With his food in hand, he left, saying nothing else. When he was in his car, he gripped the steering wheel tight and took several deep breaths to compose himself, realizing he was sweating.

He told himself it was just a bad day. He was tired and overstimulated. Maybe it was even a result of the PEP shots. Unwonted rage wasn't a side effect that he was aware of, but that didn't mean it couldn't have something to do with it. Regardless, there was no use dwelling on it. He just wanted to go home and be with his wife.

CHAPTER 6

David rubbed the tender spot on his deltoid. It was concealed by a cotton ball and a fresh bandage applied immediately after the shot. It stung a little, but the knowledge that this was his last PEP shot eased the pain considerably.

He was on his way home, having taken the evening off, a precaution in case side effects reared their ugly heads. It wouldn't be ideal trying to attend to a patient while dealing with cramps, nausea or lightheadedness.

The last blood tests had come back clear. In fact, they were perfect. By all indications David was as healthy as he'd ever been. Not just that, he actually felt great. He was alert and sharp. If he took a second to think about it, he would have noticed that his sense of smell was stronger than it had ever been. Based on all of this, the likelihood of side effects was practically nonexistent, but he was not about to pass up an evening with his wife in favor of work.

He stopped at the butcher on the way home and picked up some steaks for dinner, a plan that Amy was very enthused for when he relayed it to her on the phone. David felt his mouth water as he eyed the marbled cuts of meat displayed behind the glass case. He could practically taste the large ribeye as he pointed to it, confirming his selection to the stout man in the splotched apron behind the counter.

"Nice choice, bud," the butcher commented. "You can probably feed three people with that cut." He removed it with gloved hands and started wrapping it in the paper, adding, "Anything else?"

David selected a juicy-looking tenderloin for Amy, her go-to cut. The butcher retrieved and wrapped that one as well before ringing him up. He paid and left the shop, making one more stop at the supermarket before heading home.

It was close to dinner time when he walked in the door with the groceries. Amy greeted him with a kiss on the lips that lingered longer than the typical hello peck between married couples. David didn't object, wrapping his free hand around her waist and pulling her in as close as her pregnant belly would allow.

"Well, nice to see you too," he said.

She kissed him again, this time briefly. "Hey, I'm not used to going two weeks with no physical affection. Now that you're in the clear, the rent's coming due, mister!"

David laughed and cupped her cheek, pulling her in for another kiss.

Amy was right. They were an affectionate couple and having to dial it back for the past two weeks while they waited to make sure David was in the clear of any type of serious infection hadn't been ideal for either of them. Both had the intention of making up for lost time.

David kissed her again, intending it to be quick, but it quickly started picking up passion until Amy reluctantly broke it with a smile that her husband returned.

"Consider that a deposit," David said.

"It's a good start and I fully intend to collect the rest soon," she said with a smirk. "But first, your son and I need to eat something."

***

"Wow! You were hungry!" Amy noted in awe as she watched David take the final bite of his steak, swallowing it as easily as he did his first.

David chuckled and made sure his mouth was clear before answering. "I guess so. I'm just relieved to be done with the damn shots. Guess I worked up an appetite stressing over it these past few weeks."

Amy lowered her eyes to his plate. When he had placed it on the table, not only did it contain the ribeye, he also had cooked up green beans, a twice-baked potato and some garlic bread sprinkled with parsley and Romano cheese. It was all gone, just a pool of reddish juice left in its place.

David felt an urge to lick it up. In fact, he just now realized that he hadn't cooked it as much as he usually did. He liked his steak medium rare, but the mammoth cut of meat was taking longer to cook so he removed it from the grill before attaining the typical level of doneness he would opt for.

Fighting the urge, he pushed his plate away. He wasn't a damn animal after all. But it was odd that he was still hungry, practically impossible after all that he had consumed. He got lost in his thoughts to the point where he didn't notice Amy had gotten up from her seat and was standing next to him. She waved her hand up and down in front of his face.

"Paging Dr. Bixby."

He looked up and met her eyes. She smiled down at him.

"Sorry. I guess I zoned."

"I guess so," she acknowledged. "Food coma?"

He laughed. "No, I'm actually okay."

"Are you? I don't think I've ever seen you down that much food in one sitting."

"Me either." David was confused, but he honestly had never felt better. "I'm fine, trust me. Just eating away the stress of the last few weeks. I'll drink a lot of water and stick to salad tomorrow."

A hint of mischief curled into a smile on her face. "I'm

more curious if you'll be able to perform after all that."

David got the hint and stood up, silencing her doubts with a kiss. She returned it, but they didn't break away this time. Instead, their mouths opened and their tongues met. David could actually taste her steak as they made out. It didn't repulse him. It actually turned him on more, as if satisfying some deeper hunger.

After a few minutes of intense kissing, Amy broke away with a gasp, needing to catch her breath. David immediately felt the absence of her lips and grasped the back of her head with his left hand, pulling her in again as his right pulled down the left strap of her tank top, exposing her breast. He ran his thumb over her nipple, feeling it harden under his touch.

She pulled back again, putting a little more distance between them this time. "Whew! Need a breather, baby."

David's urges were only rising. His erection strained against his pants, crying out to be free. But he honored his wife's request and didn't push further.

"Sorry, darling," he said, having trouble concentrating on his words. "I just want you so bad."

Amy smiled. "I want you too. It's been too long. We just need to get somewhere more comfortable."

***

Moments later, they were in their bedroom. Amy led him

by the hand, guiding him back toward the bed. When she got there, she sat on the edge and pulled down the other strap of her tank top, completely exposing her breasts to him.

"You are so beautiful," David said as he leaned down and put his mouth on her nipple, circling his tongue around one before lightly grazing it with his teeth as he pulled away. He repeated the process on the other as Amy grabbed a fistful of his hair, holding him close to her.

She pushed him back, but his disappointment was only temporary as she pulled down his shorts and underwear, letting them drop to the floor as she took him in her mouth. He was painfully hard. It was almost as if he had years of pent-up sexual urges even though it had only been a couple weeks.

His head rolled back as his wife sucked him, knowing exactly how to work him with her lips and tongue. They had been sexually compatible right from the start and that familiarity was paying off now as she made him feel amazing.

"I missed this," Amy breathed as she took a moment to release him from her mouth, but not her hand which continued to stroke him.

David looked down and locked eyes with her. He saw the desire in them, which only amplified his own as she put her lips around him again. They didn't break eye contact as she continued.

He placed his hands on either side of her head, but he only rested them there, not grabbing or pulling, just moving in concert with the motion of her head. This wasn't uncommon. They could get kinky, even rough at times, but they were always aware and respectful of each other. If she objected, she would let him know.

But there was something different this time. David tightened his grip a bit. Amy didn't protest as he helped move her along. The sensations were incredible. His arousal was rocketing to levels he had never experienced. Suddenly, he felt different. Like he was watching someone else from inside his body.

He was still in control. Still didn't push further than he had, but he had an urge to pull her hair. To fuck her mouth as hard as he could. It took everything he had to not give in, but he lost the battle as felt his fist tighten on her locks. She released him and gripped his wrists gently, giving him the hint to let go.

David's brain told him not to. To grab her and pull her back until he finished, but he fought it. He let go, having much more difficulty than he should have. It worried him.

"Easy, tiger," she said. "I can't have you finishing before you fuck me."

Her dirty talk put any concerns on hold. She laid back on the bed and started pulling down her leggings. David assisted, discarding them on the floor as he lowered his own head between her legs and went to work. He knew his wife's body as well as she knew his and focusing on her provided a temporary distraction from his urges. He hit all the right spots with the right rhythm and it wasn't long until she shook with an orgasm, her own bottled-up desire from their temporary drought spilling over.

Amy barely had time to catch her breath before David was on his feet between her legs. She gasped as he plunged into her as she lay on the edge of the bed, a position they had found workable as her pregnancy progressed.

His lust-infused madness surfaced again. Her moans encouraged him at first as he picked up his pace but soon he was pounding away so furiously, romantic notions started falling away.

"Slow... down... babe," Amy said between breaths.

David heard the words but didn't want to heed them. Didn't she know it had been too long? Didn't she realize how badly he needed this? How fucking selfish could she be?

What the hell are you talking about, man? This isn't you.

Fuck that. She owed him. He needed this.

Fucking bitch.

"Babe!"

Amy's voice broke in again and David used every bit of

willpower he could muster to stop. He looked down at her. She reached up and stroked his cheek.

"I know it's been a minute, but you need to be a little gentler."

David felt sick to his stomach. He had never felt such an impulse before. Even now, he wanted to ignore her and just go back to it. How dare she keep him from finishing?

The implication of the dark thoughts terrified him. This was the person he loved most in the world. He couldn't treat her like this. He couldn't.

You can. You have to.

David took a step back, his erection aching to return as soon as it was out. He took a deep breath to calm himself. The voice was gone, but he still felt residual anger. He was afraid that if they continued, he wouldn't be able to stop, even if she wanted him to.

He turned and sat on the edge of the bed next to Amy, who worked her way first to her elbows, then to a seated position. She pulled her tank top up to cover her breasts before putting her arms around him.

"What's wrong?" she asked.

"I... I'm sorry. I got carried away."

"No kidding."

He put his head in his hands. He felt like he might cry.

"I'm sorry."

"It's okay," she said, although there was definitely a hint

of worry in her voice. "It was just a little... much."

Now he felt like throwing up. The fact that he had made his wife uncomfortable during sex was nauseating to him. It wasn't the person he was.

"I guess I'm still a little off. I really am sorry if I hurt you."

She turned his face toward hers.

"You didn't hurt me. Just wasn't used to that kind of intensity. I know it's been a while, but I'm kind of delicate right now."

She punctuated the last sentence by rubbing her stomach. His shame intensified.

"I'm sorry," was all he could muster again.

She kissed him. "Think you can go a little easier?"

No. I don't think I can.

"I think we're good for tonight," he replied.

She looked disappointed. "But you didn't..."

He stopped her. "It's all good. Let's call it a night."

She nodded in agreement, but more worry crept into her expression. She looked at him like she didn't recognize him and that broke his heart.

He excused himself to the bathroom where he masturbated, ejaculating like he could never remember before. It calmed the intrusive desires somewhat, but they lingered nonetheless. When he got back to bed, the couple exchanged a cursory kiss before rolling over in opposite directions.

It took David a very long time to fall asleep.

CHAPTER 7

David was back at work the following evening. It was only moderately busy, but David was silently thankful every time he had to see a new patient. The failed lovemaking session with Amy weighed heavily on his mind. When he didn't have to be on treating a broken bone or an elderly man with chest pains, he ended up replaying the incident in his head, the recollection nauseating him.

It wasn't just David who seemed to have an off night. Jenna was working, but something dour replaced her typical flirty demeanor. She had put no makeup on, even though she rarely used much. Her hair, normally tied back neatly, was just tossed up into a messy bun. Honestly, it was more practical than her normal style, being that they worked in a messy, often physical environment. But, for someone like Jenna, who seemed to always put effort into her appearance, the departure was quite noticeable.

But it wasn't just her physical appearance. She wore a weary look. The kind borne out of stress or anxiety. Not that David couldn't have used a break from her borderline inappropriate banter, but she looked on the verge of tears. Someone needed to make sure she was okay, if nothing else, so she could focus on the critical duties of her job.

While Jenna excused herself to go to the restroom, David flagged down Peggy, one of the older nurses who tried to take on a mentorship role with younger staff but more often than not found herself at odds with them when their work ethic didn't match her own.

"Is Jenna okay?"

"That's a loaded question, Doctor Davey."

She also had an annoying habit of assigning nicknames to people hoping they'd catch on, even though they rarely did.

"Seriously. She doesn't seem herself."

"You mean she's not all gussied up and salivating over you like prime rib?"

"Peggy."

She got the hint and softened her tone. "Yeah. She's definitely off. She was texting pretty furiously over in the break room a while ago. Thought she was going to break her damn thumbs she was tapping that thing so hard."

"Think she's having an issue with someone?"

"Probably her boyfriend. She complains about him all the time. Got out of the service a couple years back and hasn't really done much in the way of finding work from what I understand. I told her she should just dump his ass, but what does old Peggy know?"

"I knew she had a boyfriend, but I never heard her talk much about him."

"C'mon Doctor Davey, she ain't gonna talk about him in front of you."

He didn't like the implication. "What's that supposed to mean?"

"You can't tell me you don't know that girl's all hot in the britches for you?"

David frowned. "I'm not blind, Peggy. But I am married. Happily."

His thoughts returned to last night's incident, but he tried to shake it away. It was just an anomaly. He was coming off of two weeks of some pretty potent meds. It wasn't their norm. It didn't mean his marriage was in trouble.

But it didn't feel right. Not by a long shot.

"Hey, Doc, you ain't gotta convince me. I don't get involved in folks' personal lives."

David knew that wasn't true but didn't call her out on it. "Just... keep an eye on her. We can't have her distracted while she's attending to patients." Just then, he caught Jenna returning out of the corner of his eye. He grabbed a clipboard off the desk and pretended to be reviewing it with Peggy and lowered his voice as she approached. "If you think she won't be able to focus, send her home for the night."

***

Thankfully, the rest of the evening was uneventful so Jenna's lack of focus was not a major issue. She continued to check her phone, her face screwing up with expressions of anger and frustration each time. But there were no life-threatening emergencies so Peggy didn't send her home.

David was tired and ready to leave but took his time as he packed up. He wasn't necessarily avoiding going home, but he found himself ashamed to face his wife, a feeling he'd never experienced before. She'd assured him it was okay, but he knew what was in his mind and it scared him. He had always prided himself on maintaining control and discipline. He'd never struggled with it like he had last night.

Unable to delay any longer, David said goodbye to the morning staff rolling in as he exited the building. It was just after 4 a.m. so it was still dark. Halfway to his car, he stopped when he saw Jenna standing at the curb, looking at her phone.

He felt bad. She was clearly going through something, but he didn't want to engage.

She looks good.

David was surprised at the thought. He wasn't blind or an idiot. He knew Jenna was attractive by every measure, but, while he could admire her beauty, he would never cheat on his wife.

Those same eyes that found their way to Jenna's ass, admiring how it looked, even in the baggy garment.

Jesus Christ, what was wrong with him?

"Fuck!" He heard her shout, distracting him from ogling her behind.

He looked up just in time to see her turn around and make eye contact, her green eyes moistened as tears tried to fight their way out.

God damn it.

She turned around and her upper back rose and fell with a deep breath as she attempted to compose herself as if somehow David wouldn't have noticed her distress. He knew he was asking for trouble, but she was clearly in a bind and he couldn't just walk away without at least checking on her.

"Hey," he said as he approached. "Are you okay?"

She kept her back to him and uttered a weak, "Yup. All good."

He put his hand on her shoulder to gently nudge her around. The slight contact sent a charge through him. He almost recoiled at the odd sensation.

When she gave in and turned, he saw that her bloodshot eyes had lost the battle with her tears. Her lip quivered as she looked up at him, the dam threatening to burst at any moment.

"Jenna, it's obvious something's wrong. What is it?"

"I can't get an Uber."

Not surprising at this time.

"No car?"

She scoffed at the mention. "No, I have a car, but my asshole boyfriend decided it would be a good idea to drive to the bar and get absolutely obliterated with his boys."

Ah. So that explained her mood that evening. David was sympathetic but uninterested in the details. He currently had his own concerns on the domestic front.

"Sorry to hear," was the best he could come up with in his effort not to engage much further.

"Is what it is," she said as she held up her phone and waved it about as if that would somehow result in a driver accepting her ride request.

"Is there anyone else you can call?" David asked, really hoping for an affirmative.

"At this hour? Nope. Frank swore up and down that he'd be able to pick me up, but my dumb ass should have known better. He always gets fucked up when he's out with the guys," she explained before cursing at her phone. "Stupid fucking app!"

She shoved the device into her purse and looked up at David, the pleading look in her eyes telling him he was going to ask the question he hoped she wouldn't.

"David, is there *any* way you can give me a ride?"

Normally, she would have made the question a double entendre, rarely passing up an opportunity to flirt. But this time was different. She was legitimately asking for a favor. There was no subtext he was missing. She needed help and David would have felt guilty turning her down. And guilt was something he had too much of at the moment.

"How far away is your place?"

***

It was now ten to six and David leaned against the wall of his shower, trying his damnedest to choke back the sickness in his stomach as the hot water cascaded off of him. He had turned it as hot as he could stand, wanting to scald himself. Wanting to feel some pain for what he had just done.

His intentions were good. He just planned on giving her a ride and letting her off in front of her house. When she half-jokingly asked him if he wanted to come in, of course he fully meant to turn her down.

But he didn't. He said, "Sure," surprising himself and his colleague.

They didn't say another word after that and as soon as they walked through the door, they were on each other, kissing with a ferociousness he had never experienced. When she lowered to her knees and pulled off his pants, he grabbed her hair and plunged in and out of her mouth in the way he so longed to do the other night with his wife. She grabbed his buttocks and pulled him in, encouraging him to play rough.

He had felt himself rocketing toward climax so he pulled her off of him and grabbed her chin, pulling her up and kissing and licking her drool-soaked lips and chin.

The urges had peaked. He turned her around and bent her over the couch, yanking her pants down before unceremoniously ripping her panties, the thin garment tearing like tissue paper.

She had been incredibly turned on and his erection met no resistance entering her as she moaned her approval. They fucked furiously, rutting like animals until he unloaded inside of her.

David wanted to drive his fist through the tile as he bit the washcloth in an attempt to suppress his scream of rage, the reality of his infidelity hitting him like a freight train. The cheating was bad enough, but he had actually come inside of her with no protection. What the fuck had he been thinking? This wasn't him.

As the despair washed over him in tandem with the water, his stomach dropped when he heard the bathroom door open. He bit harder on the washcloth as he tried to stem his anger and shame, waiting for the new occupant to announce herself.

"Babe?" Amy's groggy voice broke the silence. "You

okay?"

David swallowed hard in an effort to compose himself. "Yeah, darling," he answered. "All good."

Except for the fact that I just stepped out on our marriage.

He heard her shuffle across the bathroom to sit down and pee.

"Sorry for interrupting," she said with a yawn. "I couldn't hold it any longer."

"No problem," he said as he suddenly felt an urge to wash the offending organ between his legs again. "I'll be out in a few minutes."

CHAPTER 8

Amy had dozed back off by the time David got into bed. Sleep wasn't even in the realm of possibility as he lay there, turned away from his pregnant wife. He no longer felt the anger and shame. Instead, numbness had permeated his body and, when Amy finally woke up, he realized he hadn't even been thinking, just staring at the digital numbers clicking away on the alarm clock on his nightstand.

When he heard her sit up, he shut his eyes, feigning sleep. When she leaned over and kissed his cheek, he felt sour bile bubble up in his throat.

She was very careful as she got out of bed and got dressed. Her ginger movements telling David she believed he was asleep. It was agonizing for him to listen to her go about her morning business. He wanted to get up and blurt out everything before begging for forgiveness.

She'll never find out. You're not the first guy to ever fuck around on his wife.

The thought jolted him. He never looked at it that way.

Sure, David knew plenty of guys who cheated, but he never got involved in analyzing or judging. He always felt what goes on in the confines of someone else's relationship was none of his business so long as it didn't affect his own.

But he had most definitely affected his own a few hours before.

When Amy finally left the room, David remained in bed with his eyes closed until he heard her car pulling out of the driveway. Knowing sleep would not bless him with its presence, he got out of bed and looked out the window to confirm Amy's car was indeed gone.

As he dressed, he saw a piece of paper scribbled with his wife's handwriting on the vanity. He picked it up and read:

Baby, I know you got home later than usual.

That first line hit his heart like a sledgehammer, almost causing him to crumple the note, but he kept reading.

I didn't want to wake you. Going for a spa day with my sister. Figured you wouldn't mind having the house to yourself on your day off. You've been working so hard, you deserve time to relax.

He didn't deserve it. And he didn't deserve her.

I love you and I'll see you tonight!

—Amy

He gently placed the paper back on the vanity and rested his hands on either side, glimpsing his bloodshot eyes in the mirror. As he stared at his sullen reflection, he was startled when he heard his phone buzz.

The screen said *UNKNOWN CALLER.*

Another fucking telemarketer. He rejected the call.

A few seconds later, it buzzed again.

UKNOWN CALLER.

He rejected it again.

He was halfway down the stairs when it buzzed a third time. This time he picked up.

"Scam someone else, asshole."

"No scam, Dr. Bixby," an oddly familiar voice said on the other line in its strange American accent.

Where had he heard that voice before?

"Who is this?"

"Detective Chaney."

He recalled the encounter with the odd "detective" down in the morgue with the guy who bit him. To be honest, once he was gone, he hadn't given him much thought, assuming he had moved on.

"*Detective,*" David said sarcastically. "Cut the shit. I know you're not police."

A pause. "Then you're smart. You're also smart enough to know that something isn't quite right with you."

David's blood chilled. Who was this guy?

"I'm feeling just fine. Goodbye."

"Don't hang up!" the man shouted into the line.

"What is this about?"

"You're changing. You're feeling something inside that you can't understand or explain," the man said, pausing again before adding, "But I can."

"Ok. I'm listening."

"Not over the phone. Meet me on the waterfront. The Salty Pelican. You know the place?"

"Yeah, I know it, but why would I meet you? You impersonated a police officer which, by my estimation, makes you a criminal. I'm not going to have a beer with you."

"This isn't a social call, Dr. Bixby. We need to talk. Today."

"So fucking talk!" David shouted, his patience gone.

"Not. On. The phone," the man replied. "Meet me at The Salty Pelican at noon."

"I told you..."

"And I told you. Meet me there at noon or I'll send these to your wife."

David froze, wondering what he meant while simultaneously knowing it could only be one thing. He felt the phone buzz against his ear as the text came through. He opened it and saw a very conclusive picture of Jenna leading him by the hand into her apartment. David was looking over his shoulder, his face was strangely blurred relative to the rest of the pic, but it was still discernibly him.

He swallowed hard as he slowly raised the phone

back to his ear, contemplating carefully how he would respond. He didn't have to. "Chaney" continued.

"I wouldn't have been able to capture these photos after tomorrow. Once the change is complete."

"What?" David asked, his head spinning to comprehend.

"I'll explain everything. The Salty Pelican. Noon."

***

David pulled up to the restaurant ten minutes before noon. It was a popular spot on the Amelia Island waterfront, an upscale resort area just outside of Jacksonville. The bar overlooked the bay where guests at the nearby Ritz Carlton could charter boats for the day to fish or lay out before scouring the shops for antiques and local trinkets.

Scanning the area before entering the building, David felt his phone buzz in his pocket as he approached the entrance. Expecting it to be Chaney, he looked at the notification only to see a text from Jenna.

Hi.

He dismissed it, considering blocking her, but that may just compel her to come to his house and that was certainly something he couldn't afford right now. It didn't matter. It was a problem for later. Right now, his primary concern was dealing with his potential blackmailer.

As he went to slide the phone back into his pocket, he felt it buzz again, sending a cold spike of irritation under the surface of his skin. This time the text was from the unknown number he'd expected.

Out back.

He walked past the hostess without making eye contact, only offering a cursory "I'm meeting someone" as she tried unsuccessfully to greet him. The day was pleasant and the bar was already filling up with patrons, which David supposed was a good thing since he and the faux detective would blend in with the crowd.

The back section was past the bar and around the corner, down a short flight of stairs. Large windows let in copious amounts of sunlight, illuminating the room that was lined with wooden tables adorned with red-and-white checkered tablecloths. The smell of fresh seafood permeated the air and suddenly David found himself starving despite his anxiety about his current predicament. A woman at a nearby table was just starting on a lobster roll and David salivated at the sight of it, resisting an urge to snatch it out of her hands and devour it in as few bites as he could.

He shook off the hunger and spotted his meeting partner at a corner table. The man was wearing a muted gray polo shirt and Bermuda shorts. The fedora he had worn at the hospital was now replaced by a matching bucket hat. His eyes were obscured by a pair of silver-rimmed aviators. He looked like a tourist trying to pass as a local.

Who was this guy?

Chaney offered no greeting as David sat down in the chair across from him. An untouched pint of amber beer sat in front of him, the foam dissipating as condensation formed a puddle on the tablecloth beneath the glass. There was a small box sealed with packaging tape tucked off to the corner.

"So, let's hear it," David said, with no intention of standing on ceremony.

Chaney took a long sip of the beer. Something about the way he gulped it down infuriated David. He envisioned punching the bottom of the glass as the man drank, shattering it into his smug fucking face, shredding the skin as glass embedded in his lips. He wouldn't even care about cutting his own hand. David imagined licking his own fucking blood when he was done, savoring the coppery taste.

What the fuck is wrong with you?

"You with me, Dr. Bixby?"

David shook as head as he came out of his trance. He saw the man staring at him.

"What?" he asked, confused.

"You looked lost for a second. Let me guess. Fantasizing about ripping my throat out?"

Not quite, but still shockingly close.

"Who are you?" David asked, getting back to business. "What's your name?"

"Chaney's fine."

"But that's not your real name, is it?"

"Not relevant."

"I say it is."

"And I say you're not in a position where you need to know it."

David sat back in his chair, the frustration rising again, threatening to bubble over.

"Then what the fuck are we doing here?"

"Do you use profanity often, Dr Bixby?"

"Fuck this," David said as he pushed his chair back, making like he was going to stand up.

But he stopped. He couldn't leave. This guy had dirt on him. The first dirt that had ever stained David in his life. What's more, he didn't typically curse. He wasn't a choirboy, but the way he was peppering swears into his vocabulary lately was just another indicator that something was not right with him.

And, out of everyone he had come into contact with in the past few weeks, this stranger was the only person who seemed to have any idea what was happening.

David pushed his chair back in and folded his hands in front of him on the table. He took a deep breath to compose himself. It helped, but barely.

"Okay. Let's talk. No, I rarely use profanity like that.

There's a lot going on with me right now that I don't understand. But you seem to know something about it, so let's hear it."

Before Chaney could answer, a waitress with curly auburn hair and a bright smile approached. David found his eyes drawn to her ass which filled out her jean shorts nicely. He envisioned bending her over the table right then and there.

"He'll have a Johnny Walker Blue, neat. Make it a double."

Once again, David was pulled from his odd thoughts by the stranger's voice. He had no intention of drinking, but the waitress departed with a smile and a "Sure thing, hon," before he could protest.

"It's a little early for Scotch," David told the man. "Especially of the high-end variety."

"Well, Doc, I wanted to buy you something special for your last drink."

David's stomach knotted at the implication. "What the hell does that mean?"

Chaney slid the box across the table. "There's a gun in there. With one bullet."

David pushed the box back to Chaney, who didn't try to ping-pong it back to him.

"Are you insane?" David whispered. "Why would you give me a fucking gun?"

Chaney remained stone-faced. "Because you need to

kill yourself."

David felt dizzy all of a sudden. He had imagined a dozen different ways this conversation would go, but this was not one of them.

"Why would I do that?"

"Because, tomorrow night, you're going to turn into a werewolf."

The bewildered doctor laughed in spite of himself, thinking this had to be a joke at this point. The theater of the absurd.

"A werewolf. Like Lon *Chaney*?" David asked, understanding the man's choice of alias for the first time.

"Yes," he answered, dead serious. He pushed the box back to David. "There's a silver bullet in the chamber. It's the only thing that will kill you."

"This is beyond crazy. You know that, right?"

"I wish it was. But it's not. Tomorrow night, you will turn into a werewolf. If your wife is with you when you do, you will kill her. Which I'd say would make you feel even worse than you do right now for cheating on her."

There it was. The reason that he didn't just laugh this whole thing off and get the hell out of there. This guy knew about Jenna.

"So, you've been following me."

"I have."

Oddly, David appreciated the frankness with which he admitted it. At least the guy wasn't going to try to bullshit him about that part.

"Why?"

"The man who bit you that night in the ER was a werewolf. He hadn't yet turned because the moon was between cycles. But it doesn't matter for you. The bite transmits the infection no matter the state of the transmitter."

"Okay. I'll play along," David said acting like he actually had a choice. "How did you know he was a werewolf?"

"Because I've been tracking him for months. I saw the real him. I knew."

Another realization smacked David in the face. One he couldn't believe hadn't come to him sooner. "You shot that man."

"Yes."

"Why?"

"He was going to turn back into a werewolf at the next full moon. Night after tomorrow."

"But I thought you said I would turn tomorrow?"

"You will."

"But you said the full moon is two nights from now."

"People with your *condition* change three nights during the moon cycle. The night before the full moon. The night of the full moon. And the night after."

"Why?"

"Don't know."

"But, how do you know so much about werewolves?"

"I wish I didn't."

For the first time, he was being evasive. David was hitting close to home with this line of inquiry.

"Are you some kind of monster hunter?"

"No. I'm just an ordinary man."

"So, why you? Why were you hunting that man?"

"It's not important."

The anger rose again, but David suppressed it. He was actually shaking as his body had a physical reaction to the conversation.

The waitress interrupted by placing the glass of Scotch in front of David. He felt his rage dissipate as he looked over the attractive woman who smiled warmly at him before turning her attention to his companion.

"You fellas ready to order?"

"Going to need a few minutes," Chaney said.

"You know," the waitress replied, "I love your accent. I had a cousin from Minnesota. Used to visit her all the time. Always enjoyed going out there. Nice to get to a bit of a cooler climate now and then."

David noticed Chaney squirm a little despite his efforts not to react. The waitress had inadvertently revealed something that this man clearly wanted kept to himself.

"We'll give you a wave when we're ready if that's okay with you," Chaney said, trying to play it off.

"All good with me, sweetie," she said before turning to David and giving him a subtle wink. "I'll be around."

David sat back in his chair and stared Chaney down incredulously.

"You want me to believe that I'm going to turn into a werewolf tomorrow night if I don't kill myself with the gun you've so kindly provided for me. Do I have that right?"

"Correct." Now his honesty was actually pissing David off, but he continued. "I don't expect you to believe me. Not completely. But I want you to think about this. You're a doctor. That wound on your hand healed in record time. Even for someone as healthy as you."

"That doesn't mean there's some supernatural explanation."

"Tell me you don't feel different. You're not angrier? You don't feel aggression like you've never felt before? Sexual urges so strong that you'll cheat on your pregnant wife?"

David didn't know what to say. Everything this man said was correct and he was mentioning all the things that were worrying him, but could his life really be about to turn into some Hollywood creature feature? Besides all that, there was one bigger question that he had to ask.

"So why don't you just kill me?"

"I'm not a murderer, Dr. Bixby."

"There's an unclaimed body in the morgue that says otherwise."

"That was different."

"How?"

"That man deserved what he got. He was evil. Maybe he wasn't always that way, but by the time I shot him, there was no good left in him. The wolf killed that. When he died, that was supposed to be the end of it, but when I saw your bite wound, I knew he had infected you. I think you're a good man, Dr. Bixby, but you will not be for much longer. I'm sorry you found yourself in this situation. You didn't ask for it any more than I did when I first got involved in this world of monsters. That's why I want to give you a chance to do the right thing."

"That's a pretty big risk considering what you believe is going to happen to me tomorrow."

"Not really. I'll be waiting nearby. I have other silver bullets. If you don't kill yourself, I'll finish the job."

A million thoughts raced through David's mind. This man had just threatened his life. He should grab him by the collar of that stupid polo shirt and yank him across the table, pummeling him unconscious before turning him in to the police.

But he didn't. Despite everything, this man had given him the only thing resembling a plausible explanation for his plight. He almost fought a woman in a restaurant. That wasn't him. He never would've fucked Jenna, no matter how strong she came on to him or how much he may have wanted to. But he did. He did it all and he couldn't control himself.

As he contemplated how to respond, Chaney threw a hundred-dollar bill on the table and stood up. He put his hand on David's shoulder in a gesture of comfort before leaving.

"I'm sorry, Dr. Bixby. There's no other way."

David sat there for several minutes after the man left, his mind racing as he looked at the unassuming box on the table next to him. Once again, he didn't notice the waitress until she was right next to him.

"You guys change your mind about eating?" she asked, a hint of disappointment in her voice.

David downed the Scotch like a shot of tequila before abruptly taking the box and leaving the restaurant without another word.

CHAPTER 9

Back home, David still had a few hours before Amy returned. He paced his office, a fresh Scotch in hand. This time, he sipped it as he stared at the box that Chaney had given him. He hadn't yet opened it, but knew he had to. He relented and ripped the cardboard apart, recoiling as the pistol fell out and hit the floor, scared that it would go off. Fortunately, it didn't.

David eyed the weapon. It was black with a brown handle, a silver circle engraved with a horse and the word *Colt* on either side of the grip. It reminded him of the guns that the old timey detectives used in those black-and-white noir thrillers.

He carefully picked it up and inspected it, cognizant of pointing the business end away from himself. Was there really a silver bullet in there? David tried to push the cylinder open, but it didn't budge. Not knowing much about guns other than what he saw on TV, it perplexed him when it didn't flop open like it always did on screen. Turning it over in his hands, he saw a knob protruding on one side. He pushed his thumb against it and slid it back, watching as it opened.

There were six chambers. Five were empty. One contained the bullet.

David turned the firearm upside down and let the bullet fall out into his other hand, confirming that it indeed appeared to be silver. His skin tingled at the feel of the metal. It was odd, but he still wasn't sure if he believed the man, but he knew for sure that the man believed it himself.

He returned the bullet to the chamber and carefully closed it before placing it in the top drawer of the oak desk that Amy had picked out for him.

The weapon stowed, he sat down at his computer and went to work. He couldn't believe the words he was about to type, but he did anyway.

Minnesota werewolf attack

The first article that came up was from 2013 about a sixteen-year-old boy who survived a wolf attack. It was the first wolf attack ever recorded in Minnesota. However, that boy was still alive and well according to the article. Plus, there was no mention of anything unusual about the wolf.

David typed in a new search.

Minnesota animal attack

Again, an article came up. The Devereaux family was driving home from visiting a relative when their car broke down in a remote area by Boundary Waters

Canoe Area Wilderness. They had been trying to beat a significant snowstorm that was about to cover the area. Unable to get cell reception, the father, Ronald Devereaux, left his family bundled in the car while he trekked several miles to the nearest gas station hoping to get a tow truck.

When they returned, his wife and three children—nine, five and two—were all dead. The report said they had been mutilated by what appeared to be a large animal. By all estimates, it was likely a grizzly bear. David scanned the article but saw no pictures of Ronald Devereaux, so he opened a new window and searched the name.

Several other articles about the attack came up, but none had pictures. David switched over from news to image search and saw a bunch of random faces, none of which matched the man who wanted him to commit suicide.

Except one.

Halfway down the page, he saw the familiar face. It looked different, primarily because he had a genuine smile in a family photo with his wife and three children, a far cry from the dour man he had just met. Clicking the link took him to a social media page where he saw many other pictures of the Devereaux family in happier times. The page was private so there wasn't much to see other than the occasional profile picture updates, but it was definitely him.

The pieces were in place except for one critical detail. There was nothing anywhere to say that it wasn't a grizzly bear. David was going through something. There was no doubt about that, but a werewolf? He wasn't going to put a bullet in his head over something he didn't believe in. Sure, he had fucked up and he had to figure a way out of it, but it wasn't going to be by suicide.

David drained the last of his Scotch and poured himself another as he stared at Ronald Devereaux on the screen. Before long, Amy's car pulled into the driveway and he felt his heart sink. His little detour with the strange man was just another secret he had to keep from her. Just another reason to feel guilty.

As if on cue to twist the knife, his phone buzzed. Another text from Jenna.

Can we talk?

He couldn't have her blow up his phone with Amy around. Not to mention, he also had a more pressing problem with Devereaux, so he punted, texting back:

Not right now. I'll talk to you at work on Sunday.

That would be the night after tomorrow when this thing would come to a head. He could deal with the consequences of his infidelity after he handled this more pressing, life-threatening situation.

But how would he deal with Devereaux without acquiescing to his insane request? He thought about calling the cops right now, but he didn't know where to send them. Worse, he knew that, even if they caught him, he would reveal everything about Jenna and he'd no longer be able to keep it from Amy. He thought about just coming clean. About everything. After all, how much further could this go? His very life was in danger. Was that worth it to keep a mistake secret?

He heard the front door open, followed by Amy's footsteps, delicate even in pregnancy, and the sound of rustling shopping bags. He deleted the incriminating text thread and shut off his phone.

"Babe? I'm home!" she announced from the other room. The sound of her voice broke his heart. He couldn't tell her. Not yet. Maybe tomorrow when Devereaux saw he wasn't going to turn into a monster. When he saw it was all a delusion, that he would let this all go and just go back to Minnesota. That was his only way to get out of this with his life and his marriage intact.

And if Devereaux didn't cooperate?

Well, if that's how things went, David would find a use for that bullet after all.

CHAPTER 10

David knew something was wrong the moment he woke up the next morning.

He felt great, but in a bad way, if that makes sense. There was a feeling of invincibility that permeated his very being. Every sound from the rustling of his sheets to the chirping of the birds outside of his window filled his ears as if they were right next to him. Every sensation down to the sheets on his body was amplified.

He stepped out of bed and walked to the window. He was shirtless, only wearing light pajama bottoms. When he looked down, he saw definition in his muscles that he hadn't seen before. His veins bulged and the blood that flowed within felt warm and soothing. Splaying his hands in front of him, they looked bigger. Maybe they weren't in reality, but there was no doubt his body was changing.

Was Devereaux right?

David turned to look at his wife, who was still sleeping, her back to him. The covers draped down around her waist and the flesh of her back, exposed by the thin nightgown she wore, was tantalizing to him. He felt an erection immediately form and he thought about ripping the sheets off and fucking her right there, whether or not she was willing.

Much like the other, increasingly vile, intrusive thoughts, this one scared him. But his better nature still fought through whatever was making him feel that way. What frightened him even more was the vision he had of ripping her throat out post coitus, staining the silver sheets with her blood as he devoured her flesh.

He grabbed fistfuls of his hair and yanked hard, trying to right his mind.

It didn't work. He saw another vision. This time of himself as a giant wolf, standing on two legs, hunched over his mutilated wife. It plunged its claws into her belly, ripping it open. As she died, choking on her own blood, the wolf reached into the gaping cavity and pulled out the baby inside. The infant cried its first and last cry as the wolf brought it to its mouth, opening it wide before...

"*NO!*"

David's shout startled Amy and she bolted up in bed, confused and disoriented. She shook off her sleep when she saw her husband standing by the window. The look in her eyes told him she feared what she saw.

"David?" she asked in a panic as she struggled out of bed. "What's wrong?"

She walked around the bed and reached out to him, but he grabbed her arms, her face registering the shock as he gripped them tight.

"Ow! That hurts!"

David ignored her and held tight. One of his fingernails dug into the tender flesh, drawing a trickle of blood that he smelled immediately, the scent intoxicating and arousing him. Amy's eyes watered.

"What the hell is wrong with you?" she asked, more frightened than angry.

"I... I can't... I don't know..."

"You're not making sense!"

The tears were flowing now as her terror rose. David continued to struggle to get the words out, finally managing a semi-coherent sentence.

"You need to leave. Now."

"What are you talking about?" she responded as she again failed to extricate herself from his grip.

"I can't get into it. But you need to trust me. Pack a bag and go to your sister's house."

"Why?"

"Because if you stay, something bad is going to happen."

"David, I don't understand. What is wrong with you?"

He finally released her, shoving her back. Somehow, she maintained her balance by bracing herself on the dresser.

"I don't understand," she repeated as David made his way to the closet, pulling out a suitcase and flinging it open onto the bed.

"You don't have to. You just need to go," he said as he started emptying clothes from her drawers into the suitcase, not paying attention to what garments he was actually selecting.

"David, you need to stop right now and tell me exactly what the fuck is going on. I'm not going anywhere."

He stopped and sighed heavily, trying to compose himself. He had hoped he wouldn't have to go where he was about to go.

"I fucked Jenna."

Amy's mouth went agape. She looked like she wanted to scream, but none came out. David felt like that expression might freeze on her face for the rest of her life. A life that he was thinking would be very short if she didn't leave.

Finally, Amy spoke. "You what?"

"The other night. I came home late because I drove Jenna home and fucked her brains out. She even sucked my dick before I bent her over the couch and came inside of her."

Each word stung his throat like the worst case of acid reflux he'd ever experienced. Amy's face twisted into the most horrific expression of revulsion, betrayal and anguish that he could possibly imagine. It broke his heart even as he felt it hardening into something inhuman. But he needed her to leave and hitting her with this confession was the only way he could see to get her out of there.

She charged him and started pummeling his chest with balled-up fists. Each blow landed with as much power as she could muster, but David didn't even register the pain. He allowed her to rage for a moment before he grabbed her wrists and pushed her back again. Her expression said that she wanted to continue the assault, but it also registered fear at the look that he gave her. She slumped back to sit at the vanity. Amy lowered her head into her hands and sobbed in a way that David had never heard before.

"Why? Why would you do this to us?" she choked out as she cried.

"I'm sorry," was all he could offer. "But you need to leave. Now."

***

Thirty minutes later, David was pacing in his study when he heard the front door slam. He separated the blinds with his fingers and watched as his wife hurried to her car, head hung low, probably so none of the neighbors would see her red and sorrowful face. When the car backed out of the driveway and peeled off down the road, David let the blinds fall and sat down behind his desk.

He opened the top drawer and retrieved Devereaux's gun, popping the cylinder open again and extricating the bullet, holding it up to the light of his desk lamp. Returning the ammunition to the weapon, he sat still for several minutes before raising it to his temple. The steel felt cold against his skin, which was starting to burn. It wasn't necessarily an uncomfortable sensation, but it was one that was foreign to him. He cocked back the hammer and placed his finger on the trigger.

CHAPTER 11

David couldn't pinpoint just how long he sat at his desk, the gun pressed against his temple, but it was a very long time. He could feel his body at war with itself. Every sensation, each pulse, was vivid and pronounced. He saw the shadows outside moving between the slits of the blinds as the sun began its descent. There was no doubt that a change was happening inside. For the first time, he truly believed Ronald Devereaux.

The way he thought about assaulting and murdering his wife, the person he loved more than anything in the world, the person he had betrayed so unforgivably, was toxic to him, poisoning his heart as he felt humanity slipping away. If the thought of turning into a murderous monster wasn't enough to make him want to kill himself, the knowledge of what he had done to her, how he had hurt her, may have been enough to push him over the edge.

Still, he just couldn't do it. Maybe there was another way out. Amy was gone. There was no longer anyone to hurt in the house. If he just stayed locked in his house, the change, if it happened, would affect him alone. Once he turned back, he could look into a cure. He was a doctor, after all. He could work with his colleagues on research. They could put a team together to fix all this. When that was done, he could explain it all to Amy. She would understand that it wasn't him. It was the infection.

Yeah. That's what he would do. Fuck Devereaux. He had been weak. Too weak to protect his family. David wouldn't make the same mistake. He would survive this then he'd fix his marriage.

He returned the gun to his top drawer and once again looked out the window. Dusk was quickly approaching. If this was going to happen, it was going to happen soon.

David figured his office wasn't the best place for the transformation to happen. He needed somewhere more secure. No windows, and limited exit routes. The basement.

As he left his office and started toward the basement door, it startled David when he heard the doorbell ring.

Fuck. It was Devereaux, come to make good on his promise.

Well, let's see you try motherfucker.

David ran back to his office and took the gun from his desk before heading over to the window and carefully parting the blinds as he had earlier in the day, the sun now gone over the horizon. The person on the other side was now pounding furiously on the door, demanding entry.

Only it wasn't Devereaux.

The man pounding on his door was big. About six three and solidly built, muscles bulging out of the sleeves of his black Metallica T-shirt. His sandy hair was close-cropped in a tight fade and a long but well-groomed beard covered his face. A look of unbridled rage masked his face as he assaulted David's front door.

David had never seen him before, but he recognized the woman behind him. Jenna.

She stood there with her arms crossed below her chest, tears spilling out of her eyes, one of which sported a developing bruise. He couldn't hear what she was saying, but it seemed pretty clear she was pleading with him to stop.

Clearly, this was not a welcome development. David opted to keep the gun as he slowly crept out of his office toward the front door, careful not to expose himself through any of the windows as the thunderous knocking continued.

As he got closer to the door, the muffled yells became audible. In fact, they sounded just like they were in the room with him.

"Get out here, motherfucker!" the incensed man shouted. "You think you can fuck my girl and get away with it? I'll fucking kill you, bro! Get out here!"

"Please, Frank! Stop! It's not what you think!"

"Shut the fuck up, bitch! I saw your texts!"

"You put a bullshit tracker app on my phone! It's not even accurate! Those were fake messages!"

"Fuck you, you lying whore!"

Tracker app? David thought. He hadn't even looked at his phone since the morning. He pulled it out and saw a bevy of notifications from Jenna.

I know U said we'd talk Sun, but I can't stop thinking about you.

U probably think the other night was a mistake, but I don't. It was amazing.

I love u.

Jesus Christ, she had gone off the deep end. What did she think? He was going to leave his pregnant wife for her? How disconnected from reality could she be?

There were two more texts.

OMG. Frank knows. I don't know how, but he knows. He's coming to UR house.

Now he was here and ready to fight. David thought about opening up the door and laying him out. As strong as he felt right now, this fucker wouldn't stand a chance, it didn't matter how big he was. How dare he come to David's house looking for trouble?

David was about to open the door and confront him when a sudden stabbing pain shot through his stomach. Suddenly, it felt like every nerve ending in his body fired at once and he dropped to his knees, the gun hitting the ground and sliding under the bench in the foyer and out of reach.

The pounding and cursing on the other side of the door continued at full force. It was clear that this man wasn't going to go away. He'd come here looking for trouble and wasn't going to leave until he found it.

He was about to find it.

CHAPTER 12

Outside the house, Frank started kicking the door, but it was a heavy fiberglass model so it wasn't giving, no matter how angry the man was.

"Motherfucker!" he yelled, adding to the lengthy list of expletives spewing from his mouth.

Behind him, Jenna pleaded with him to stop, leaping toward him in an attempt to restrain him, but stepping back at the last moment, no doubt fearful of being hit.

"Stop! Police!" a voice came from nearby.

Frank turned as Devereaux approached him, dressed in the same baggy pinstripe suit he had worn to the hospital. He held out his forged police badge in front of him as he approached.

The raging man halted his assault on the door and turned.

"Back away," Devereaux said, reaching inside his jacket.

Frank complied and took a step back from the door, putting his hands out in front of him. "Listen, officer..." he started.

"No! You listen! There's an active investigation in this neighborhood. You need to leave the scene immediately."

His focus was on Frank so he didn't see the realization hit Jenna.

"You're not a cop! You're that guy that was snooping around the hospital a few weeks back."

Devereaux froze obviously having failed to consider that Jenna would recognize him. Not that it mattered. He needed to get these people out of here now and confronting them was the only way he could do that.

The hesitation was all Frank needed as he charged the police impersonator. Devereaux managed to get the pistol out of his shoulder holster but did not have time to aim as the large man speared him to the ground. Despite the impact, he maintained his grip on the gun. That is, until Frank kicked it out of his hand, sending it flying a good distance before it slid under a Jeep parked on the street.

Devereaux tried to sit up but was met with a right cross that sent his head smacking against the pavement. The next time he rose was not of his own volition, but Frank's, who yanked him up by his collar only to punch him again, sending a spray of blood to the concrete below.

Frank pulled him up for another punch, but never landed it. Instead, all three participants in the melee found their attention drawn to David's front door. A giant thud reverberated from the other side of the door. Frank and Jenna registered confusion while Devereaux's expression twisted into the horror of realization that he was too late.

Another crash pushed the heavy door forward into the frame, which splintered. Whatever was hitting it from the other side carried a great deal more impact than Frank's kicks.

The third collision left the doorframe in a precarious state, hanging by a thread.

A fourth knocked it off the hinges completely, sending the door crashing to the walkway in front of the house.

Inside, there was darkness. Followed by a low animal growl. Frank stepped up and off the battered man below and took a tentative step toward the ripped-open entryway.

"Don't..." Devereaux said in a cracked voice, barely audible even if the other two were focused on him.

For a split second, a pair of yellow eyes materialized in the blackness. Before anyone had a chance to discern what they were attached to, the werewolf leaped forward and crashed into Frank, just as he had done to Devereaux a few minutes before. Only the monster dwarfed the large man—he was almost a foot taller and a couple hundred pounds heavier.

The beast took all of Frank's wind and he couldn't even scream before it lowered its jaws onto his throat, clamping down as the skin offered minimal resistance. The creature shook its head violently as it gripped his flesh. A scream finally came, this time from Jenna, as the wolf reared back its head, taking most of Frank's neck with it as strings of mangled tendons tried to hold it in place. A geyser of blood erupted, coating the faces of the werewolf and its victim in a crimson mask.

Jenna's cries continued, with the unintended consequence of drawing the wolf's attention. It stared her down and snarled, blood and drool dripping from its mouth onto the ruined body of her boyfriend. She retreated slowly, as if that would somehow prevent the creature from pouncing, but she didn't make it far before backing into the SUV parked behind her on the curb. She pressed into it as hard as she could, as if she could somehow phase through into the safety of the interior.

The wolf roared and jumped on her, sinking its teeth unceremoniously into her left shoulder, her clavicle cracking under the force of the monster's powerful bite. As she screamed in an amalgam of fear and agony, the crack of a gunshot echoed into the night as the beast felt the bullet whiz by the back of its head.

Jenna crumpled to the ground as the wolf released her, a pool of blood forming underneath her mutilated body almost instantly. The monster that used to be David Bixby turned its attention to the direction of the gunshot, seeing Devereaux lying on the ground, braced on one elbow as he aimed the gun with shaky hands in the wolf's direction. Recognizing the danger, it didn't lunge toward the downed man. Instead, it growled and ran off in the opposite direction, barely avoiding another bullet.

Devereaux cursed as he struggled to his feet, his head pounding and spinning in concert as he tried to steady himself, likely the victim of a concussion. He stumbled over to the massacred bodies of Frank and Jenna, as he heard a howl off in the distance. The neighborhood was on a cul-de-sac backed up to the woods. The werewolf was now in its natural habitat, which would make it that much more dangerous to track. Devereaux steeled himself and followed the monster into the trees.

CHAPTER 13

The werewolf stalked its way through the woods. It could still taste the flesh of its prey on its tongue, but its hunger was nowhere near satiated. Feeding was all it cared about now.

It didn't take long for it to pick up a scent. The creature had no knowledge of what it actually was, but if David Bixby had still been in control, he would have recognized the aroma of barbequed meat permeating the air. For the wolf with its supercharged senses, it was a beacon pushing it forward.

The wolf picked up speed as it moved toward the alluring smell. The trees gave way to a clearing and it saw its next meal.

A man was standing outside of a double-wide trailer parked among several similar vehicles spread throughout the open space outside the woods. He lifted the lid on a small charcoal grill that smoked and sizzled as he flipped a full rack of spareribs atop it. The redolence filled the beast's nostrils and stimulated its salivary glands. It was time to feed.

The werewolf burst from the trees and was on the man before he could react; as the grill tumbled over, some of the burning coals landed on the wolf's leg, searing the flesh and fur. The pain was there, but in its feeding frenzy the animal paid it no mind.

It thrust both claws into the man's stomach and ripped it open like a fleshy Christmas present. The man screamed at a pitch high enough to crack glass as the wolf pulled a yard of intestine from the gaping hole and took a generous bite. The man died as the wolf lowered its snout into his abdomen and greedily devoured his bowels.

Again, a gunshot interrupted the wolf's feast. Only this time, it was from a rifle. It pulled its head from the hollowed cavity of its victim's midsection and looked up to see a heavyset, sweaty man aiming a twenty-two in the wolf's direction with shaking hands, his eyes betraying that he knew he'd fucked up by drawing the monster's attention.

The wolf leaped forward breaking into an instant run as the terrified man fired again. This time the bullet penetrated the beast's shoulder but failed to slow him much at all. With the werewolf too close for him to get off a third shot, the doomed fool tried to turn and run, but before he could take two steps, four hundred plus pounds of muscle and fur sent him crashing face first into the ground.

He felt his nose crack as he hit the dirt below

with nothing to brace himself. Blood pooled up almost instantly, filling the prone man's mouth. He wouldn't live to appreciate the fact that he could at least feel his nose, something that he couldn't do with his lower body when the werewolf shattered his spine on impact. But even that wouldn't be a concern for the soon to be dead man because the wolf clamped its jaws on his skull, cracking it like an egg as the bone caved inward, penetrating the soft brain matter below.

There were no other distractions as the wolf finished dining on the insides of the two unfortunate bystanders. David Bixby, buried deep within the creature's consciousness, would figure that any other denizens of the trailer park would be smart enough to stay barricaded in their mobile homes.

Its hunger satisfied for the moment, the wolf started making its way around the trailers. Now that it had fed, it needed to find an appropriate place to rest. As it passed around the back of a yellow single-wide with maroon curtains, it heard a wailing sound. A human would recognize it as a baby's cry, but the wolf knew it to be something else.

Dessert.

The werewolf stood fully upright and smashed its claw into the window, the glass offering no resistance as it exploded inward. More screams emanated from inside, belonging to an older child and an adult female. The wolf's hunger returned as it heard their terror.

It stuck its face through the window and saw the woman clutching a bundle of wailing meat swaddled in a light-blue blanket. She wore a pink robe and rollers in her hair. Her other hand was wrapped around a crying child about five years old. The little girl buried her face in her mother's robe, not wanting to look at the monster trying to get through their window.

Entering through the small opening was not a possibility for the lycanthrope because of its size, and it figured that out quickly. It stalked slowly along the edge of the trailer until it reached the front. There was more glass, but the opening would be much bigger once it broke through. It'd be feeding on the trio within seconds.

The wolf leaped onto the hood, the vehicle creaking and groaning under its weight as the front hood collapsed into the engine. It let out a thunderous roar as it brought its fists down in a double axe handle maneuver through the windshield. It was a different type of glass, that cracked instead of shattered. The wolf repeated the move and this time the entire structure fell into the vehicle, leaving it with the opening it needed.

The woman pulled her family to the rear of the vehicle as the wolf started to move in. She handed the infant to the older child and told her to crawl through the window with the baby and run. The girl screamed and cried and shook her head, too terrified to even move.

"There's no time!" the mom screamed as she tried to push her child to the window.

But another gunshot echoed through the night. The wolf suspended its entry into the trailer and turned toward the shot that had missed again. It saw Devereaux, stumbling out from behind another trailer, gun aimed.

He fired again, but was shooting desperately, which, when combined with his concussion symptoms, had no chance of success.

Still, the wolf recognized the danger and jumped off the hood, making a beeline for the trees as Devereaux fired again unsuccessfully. It was strange. The wolf didn't hesitate to attack the man with the rifle, but somehow it knew the weapon this man had was different. Whether that was David Bixby's influence seeping into his lupine form or just some kind of mysterious survival instinct didn't matter.

It was time for the wolf to seek shelter.

***

The noise and commotion from the trailer park died down as the werewolf moved deeper into the woods. Its hunger had again faded and it felt very tired. The burns on its legs and the bullet wound in its shoulder were now registering the pain which was getting worse as it moved. Finding a place to rest safely was its only instinct now.

It had moved a few miles in when it found an opening into a small cave. The werewolf ducked and squeezed inside. This would do.

***

Ronald Devereaux saw the cave thirty minutes after the wolf entered. He had been able to follow the blood trail, which was a mix of the wolf's shoulder wound and the dripping gore of its victims. There was no doubt it was inside. It was time to end this.

He kept his gun in front of him as he carefully stepped inside.

A gunshot echoed from within.

Devereaux screamed.

The wolf howled.

CHAPTER 14

David opened his eyes slowly. He couldn't see a damn thing and, at first, thought he had gone blind. He blinked several times and finally managed to focus on a sliver of light poking in through a hole about twenty yards away.

His eyes adjusted and he was able to make out some of his surroundings. He was in a cave. The ground below was dirty and cold. The sensation made David very aware that he was naked. He pushed himself up to a sitting position, leaning himself back against the stone wall.

He swallowed hard, his throat dry and irritated. A foul taste accompanied the saliva as it slid back down his throat. That was when everything came back to him.

The gun.

Jenna and her boyfriend.

Devereaux trying to intervene.

The bodies. So many bodies.

David grinded his teeth and clenched his fists as the guilt crushed his soul. Devereaux had been right. If he had pulled that fucking trigger, none of this would have happened.

It didn't matter. It had happened and he was damned.

His internal self-flagellation was put on hold when he heard a moan from across the cave. He turned in that direction, squinting his eyes to make out the figure in front of him.

Ronald Devereaux came into view. More accurately, what was left of Ronald Devereaux.

He, like David, sat against the wall. His face was shredded with deep gashes that ran from the right side of his forehead to the left side of his jaw. His right eye was missing, only a hollow cavity in its place. The left part of his lower lip was torn away, his gums and broken teeth clearly visible.

Another slash ran the opposite way down his chest to his abdomen. His shirt was ripped open and his innards were slowly seeping out from the gashes. As for his limbs, well, there were only two of the four remaining. His left leg was missing below the knee, the jagged bone protruding. The right arm was detached from the shoulder, the full extent of the mutilation hidden under the jagged remains of his jacket.

The man was breathing, but it was shallow and labored. He didn't have long.

"Didn't plan for your friends to show up like that."

Devereaux's words broke David's trance.

"I should have listened to you."

"Yeah, you should have," Devereaux said, his familiar

JAMES KAINE

bluntness shining through even in his final moments.

David looked around, not even sure for what. Even if he had medical equipment, there was no way he could save him. He saw the pistol against the wall opposite Devereaux. He crawled forward and picked it up, sitting back against the wall so he could face the dying man.

"I'm sorry," he said.

"You and me both, Doc."

David gripped the gun and put his finger on the trigger.

"Is this ready to fire? Any safety?"

Devereaux tried to shake his head, but it barely moved an inch.

"Safety's off."

David raised it and pressed the barrel to his temple. He closed his eyes and thought of Amy.

The first time he saw her.

Their first date.

Their first kiss.

The first time they made love.

The day they got married.

The day she told him he was going to be a father.

He finally cried now, mourning the loss of the life he was supposed to have with his wife and son. A son who would never know his dad. He'd grow up thinking that his father cheated on his mother. That he was a murderer. He'd curse him as a monster. Amy would remarry and move on with her life. She would die in love with someone else, her first husband reduced to a vile memory.

David gritted his teeth and pulled the trigger.

The gun clicked but didn't fire.

He pulled the trigger again. And again. And again. Each time the click of the empty weapon taunted him. David screamed and threw the gun across the cave, burying his head in his hands.

"I thought it might be empty but didn't want to discourage you, just in case," Devereaux said.

"What the hell am I going to do?"

"No offense, Doc, but that's a you problem. I did what I could. In retrospect, probably should have just shot you when you were leaving the hospital."

"Why didn't you?"

"I'm not a killer. I killed a monster, but never a man. You weren't a monster yet."

"Well, that was foolish of you."

"No shit."

"You don't have much longer."

"I hope not. I'm eager to see Addie and the kids. You believe in heaven, Doc?"

"I did. Now I'm not so sure. I know one thing, though."

"What's that?"

"If that's where you end up, you're never going to see me there."

CHAPTER 15

David sat with Ronald Devereaux until he died. It seemed like the right thing to do. When the former doctor confirmed that the man no longer had a pulse, he removed his clothes. They were shredded to shit and would certainly arouse suspicion in public, but, seeing as David was naked, there wasn't much choice.

Devereaux's wallet was in his pants and intact. It contained cash, credit cards and a room key for a motel a few miles away. Luckily, he had kept it in the paper sleeve with the room number written on it.

Room 124.

David made it to the motel a little before noon. He snuck his way undetected into Devereaux's room. There he was able to shower and change into clothes that didn't look like they'd been put in a blender. The dead man was a few inches shorter, so they were definitely small on him, but they would do for now.

He scoured the room for more silver bullets, but there were none to be found. The safe in the closet was locked tight, but he didn't know the code and he couldn't risk calling the front desk in case they asked for ID. He and Devereaux looked nothing alike and it would be very bad if the police got involved. Especially considering, if what the man told him was correct, he'd experience the transformation again each of the next two nights.

One thing was for sure, David wasn't going to be able to get silver bullets before then—nor likely and time soon—so he had to make sure he wouldn't harm anyone else.

Hoofing it to the nearest hardware store, David purchased heavy-duty chains and padlocks before returning to the woods and stripping his clothes. It was difficult, but he managed to wrap the chains around the tree and himself before securing it with three different padlocks. He prayed to God that it would be enough to hold the wolf.

***

David awoke the next morning, still chained to the tree. He dug the keys out of the hole he buried them into by his side and freed himself. The chains had held and, better yet, no one had come across him after he'd turned. He remembered the sensations of losing himself. The pain, like every hair follicle was on fire as it sprang from his skin. The way his bones cracked and reformed as he grew. It was like some vivid, horrible dream. The tree and soil below were covered in massive scratch marks from his attempts to escape.

He assumed that any hunt for the animal that attacked the trailer park would be during the day and people would be too scared at night to venture too far into the forest.

He laid low in the motel until just before dusk when he repeated the process again.

After he freed himself, he went back to the motel for the last time, taking Devereaux's suitcase with him. He made sure to check out before he left. Devereaux's body was still in the cave and he figured he'd be able to use his credit cards until someone reported him missing.

Unsure of his next move, David knew he had to leave Florida immediately. He had less than a month before he turned again. He had to figure out something before that happened. No one else could get hurt because of him.

***

Welcome to Georgia. We're Glad Georgia's on Your Mind.
David's eyes moistened as he read the sign while crossing state lines. He had lived in Florida his whole life, but it wasn't the locale he would mourn. He had hurt his family in ways that would likely never heal. His life was shattered by circumstances no one could ever foresee. He had just tried to help a dying man and was cursed as

a result.

Now, all he had left was to try to find a way to stop this. He was probably a wanted man and, even if he wasn't, he had no idea how to get silver bullets. Nor did he know if a silver knife would work. Could he cut his own wrists? His throat? Would that be enough?

No, David felt his best chance was to find someone who could help. There had to be a way to cure this. Maybe, if he could find a way to control it, he could explain it. Amy would understand. They could move past this. They could rebuild.

If there was a chance, David had to find it.

Chapter 16

David found Dr. Rajesh Patel walking across Princeton University campus a little before three p.m. on Thursday. He called out to him, and when the professor turned and saw the slightly unkempt man running toward him, David could only imagine what he thought. He was dressed in casual clothing and his hair had grown out quite a bit over the past few months. David had done his best to style it, but it was quite unruly and grew pretty fast these days. He had also grown out his beard which was also quite bushy since he had been on the run. He couldn't stand it but figured it best to change his appearance as much as he could.

Rajesh held up his hand, signaling for David to stop where he was and not to encroach further on his space.

"Dr. Patel," David said, "I was wondering if I could have a moment of your time."

"Are you a student?"

"No, I'm a researcher."

"A researcher. Well, you can make an appointment with my secretary. If you call the main office, I'm sure we can set something up."

"Please!" David said more desperately than he intended. "I'm here about the Genesis Project."

"Excuse me?" Patel said, his eyes bulging. "I don't know what you're speaking about."

"Please, Dr. Patel, Anna Martin sent me."

"Dr. Martin? How do you know her?"

"She was working with me on a cure."

"A cure?"

"For an affliction unlike anything anyone has ever seen."

***

An hour later, David and Dr. Patel sat across from each other in a corner booth at the Alchemist and Barrister. They ordered some drinks and food. David devoured his burger as they spoke, but Patel barely touched his own plate. He was more interested in interrogating this odd man who had inserted himself into his day.

"Dr. Martin and I conceptualized the Genesis Project years ago, but it never really got off the ground. It was mostly theoretical. Could animal genes be spliced with humans to ward off disease, increase performance or heighten senses? But it wasn't anything serious. We came up with a silly name. Book of Genesis. New life. Ha ha."

"But you had to learn something, no? Dr. Martin was

still working on similar theories."

"Yes, well, Dr. Martin always had quite a more vivid imagination than I. She always took it so much more seriously than I did. Understand, we never even made it to anything close to a trial. I think Anna may have oversold you on what we actually accomplished, which is essentially nothing."

David felt frustrated at the lack of info. When he came across Anna Martin and her research, she was so enthusiastic about the possibility of mixing the best parts of humans and various animal species. He wondered if that could truly be the source of this whole nightmare. Because if he could find the source, he could find the cure.

His frustration was giving way to anger. He wanted to flip the fucking table.

God damn it. It was too close to the full moon. Tomorrow he would turn again. He knew he wouldn't be cured by then, but he thought he could have at least made some progress. The fact that he was now taking a step back was infuriating.

"I'm sorry, sir. There really is nothing there."

David pushed back in his seat and sighed. "Still, you put in some work on this. Did you come across any colleagues who were doing similar research?"

"Why is this so important to you?"

"Because something happened that I can't explain. I

can't go into it, but your research is the only chance I have of fixing it."

He didn't know if the academic across from him believed that, but he must have seen something in his expression that told him that David needed this answer.

"Look," Rajesh said, "I don't know much. I can't emphasize enough that we made no progress on this front at all. That said, I've heard rumors of a lab in Vancouver that is engaging in research of this nature."

David brightened up. Hope crept back into him.

"Where in Vancouver?"

"I don't know. I don't even know if it's true. That's all I can offer you. I'm sorry." Patel got up and threw a hundred-dollar bill on the table. "Keep whatever change is left after the tip. Something tells me you can use it."

David looked at the man but said nothing. He simply nodded.

He finished his meal and left the restaurant, taking the hundred and not paying the bill. Pulling the old dine-and-ditch didn't feel great, but that was the least of his sins right now and he was going to need money to get to Canada. Although, how he was going to cross the border as a wanted murderer was the main issue.

But that was a problem for tomorrow. Right now, he needed to scout out a new location to hide.

When David had looked into New Jersey before arriving in the state, he found a town called Hillcrest that was filled with wooded areas, hopefully with a good hiding spot to ride out the next seventy-two hours.

The next day, he found the perfect spot. There was a cave that looked like it would be too small for the wolf to get out, even if it broke through the heavy-duty steel collar he would affix to the wall.

When dusk approached the following evening, David made his way to his hiding spot. He had prepped it with the collar, so all that was left was for him to strip down, stow the key and lock the collar around his neck.

Once the preparations were complete, he sat and waited for the change to overtake him. When this cycle was over, he would get to Vancouver somehow.

He was going to beat this.

EPILOGUE

"Brady," the boy across from him said.

David looked at him like he had two heads. This little shit had been holding him hostage for the past two days. When he had locked himself in this cave, he thought it had been the perfect hiding spot, but apparently not, since some stupid teenager decided to barge in looking for the same kid that was facing him now.

The dumbass had gotten too close and the wolf had eviscerated him. This other kid had come in after and cleaned up the crime scene before disposing of the body but hadn't let him out. He told him he was trying to figure out what was going on before deciding to release him, but David suspected he had other motives.

"My name's Brady," the kid repeated.

"Now why would you tell me your name?"

"Call it a show of good faith."

Good faith. Sure.

"Well, Brady, you don't need to know my name."

David could tell that pissed Brady off. Did he really think getting all personable would—what?—compel him to open up like they were old friends? Sure, kid.

"Fine. If you're not going to tell me your name, I'll just give you one."

"And what name are you going to give me?"

The boy smirked.

"Gunther."

Afterword

Poor David.

Now that you've experienced Gunther's tragic origin, see what happens next in *My Pet Werewolf.* If you think the shit hit the fan in this one, you haven't seen anything yet! *My Pet Werewolf* is available on Kindle, Kindle Unlimited and in paperback and hardcover formats, so you can continue the story right away!

If you want some free books, please consider joining my VIP Readers Club! If you sign up you will get two free eBooks right away as well as any I may offer in the future, updates on new projects and opportunities to participate in contests and giveaways! You can unsubscribe at any time and still keep the books! Sign up today at **www.jameskaine.net**

Also, If you enjoyed this book and have a minute to spare, please consider writing a review. Reviews help indie books like this one get in the hands of fellow readers and are very much appreciated. You can review *Gunther* on Amazon, GoodReads and BookBub.

Lastly, feel free to give me a follow on social media for updates and hot takes like regular stuff OREOs are superior to all other stuffing levels! Thank you again and I hope to see you soon!

ALSO BY JAMES KAINE

Pursuit
My Pet Werewolf
The Dead Children's Playground

ABOUT THE AUTHOR

 James Kaine picked up a copy of *The Scariest Stories You've Ever Heard* at a scholastic book fair when he was a kid and hasn't looked back since. Now an active Member of the Horror Writers Association, James, as he puts it, "lives his dream to give you nightmares." His work includes novels such as *My Pet Werewolf, Pursuit* and *The Dead Children's Playground.*

Born and raised in Trenton, NJ, James still resides in the Garden State with his wife, two children and a loveable Boston Terrier, named Obi. When not writing about horrible things, James enjoys reading, movies, music, cooking and rooting for the New York Giants. Well, maybe he doesn't enjoy that last one.

Visit www.jameskaine.net for news, info on all his books – including signed copies – or to pick up some sweet merch.

Printed in Great Britain
by Amazon

42458382R00078